SQUIDDING AROUND

FISH FEUD!

KEVIN SHERRY

WITH COLOR BY WES DZIOBA

graphix

AN IMPRINT OF

■SCHOLASTIC

To my niece Amelia
with love from your Cod-father

All rights reserved. Published by Graphix, an imprint of Scholastic Inc.,
Publishers since 1920. SCHOLASTIC, GRAPHIX, and associated logos are
trademarks and/or registered trademarks of Scholastic Inc.

The publisher does not have any control over and does not assume
any responsibility for author or third-party websites or their content.

Library of Congress Cataloging-in-Publication Data Available

ISBN 978-1-338-63668-0 (hardcover)
ISBN 978-1-338-63667-3 (paperback)

10 9 8 7 6 5 4 3 2   20 21 22 23 24

Printed in China   62

First edition, September 2020
Edited by Jenne Abramowitz
Book design by Steve Ponzo
Creative Director: Phil Falco
Publisher: David Saylor

CHAPTER 1

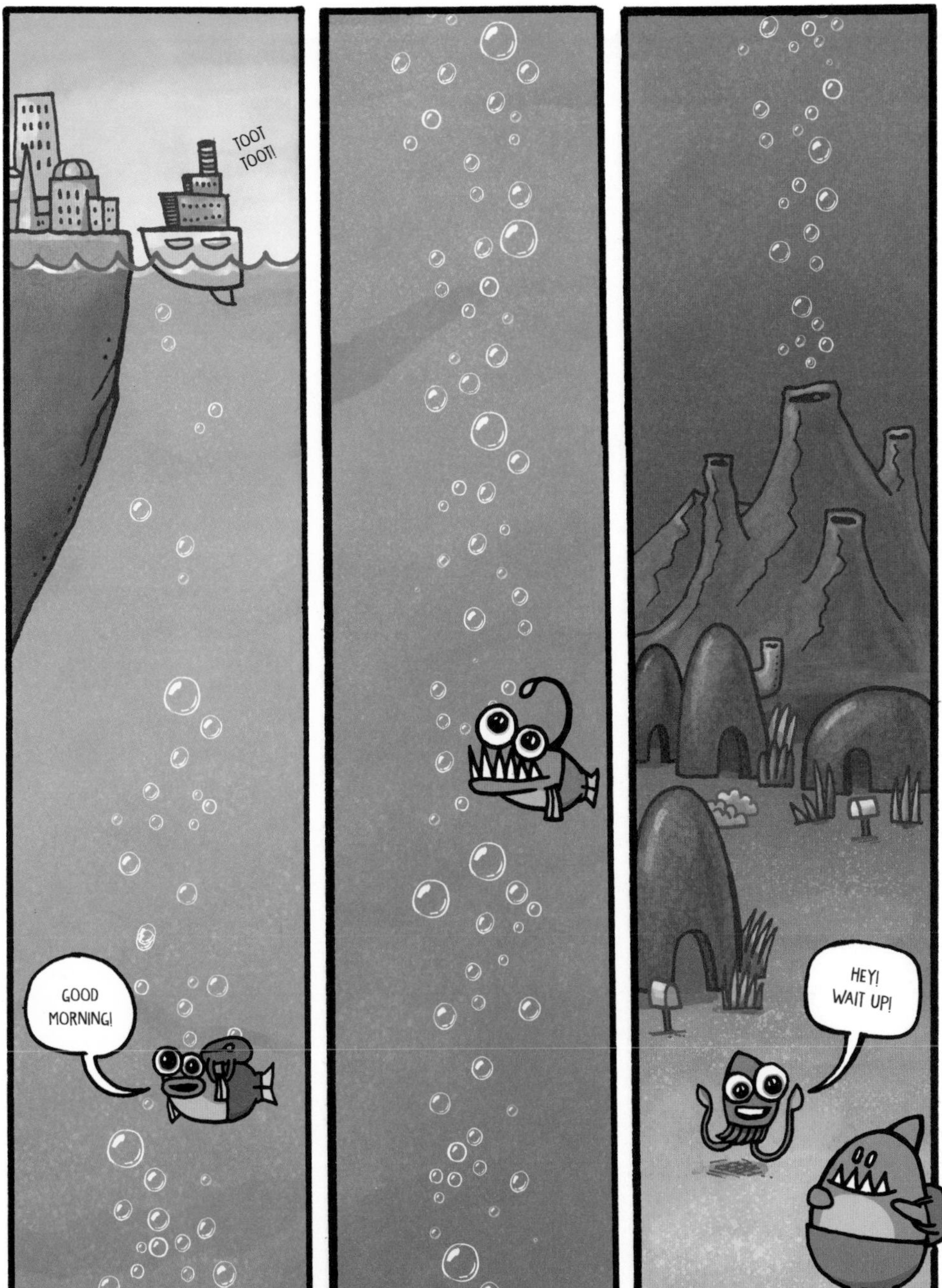
TOOT TOOT!
GOOD MORNING!
HEY! WAIT UP!

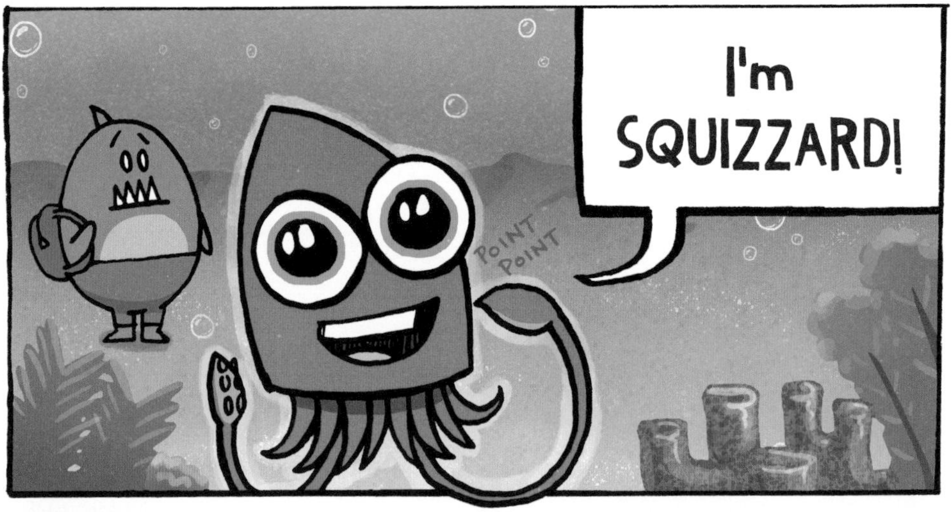
I'm SQUIZZARD!
POINT POINT

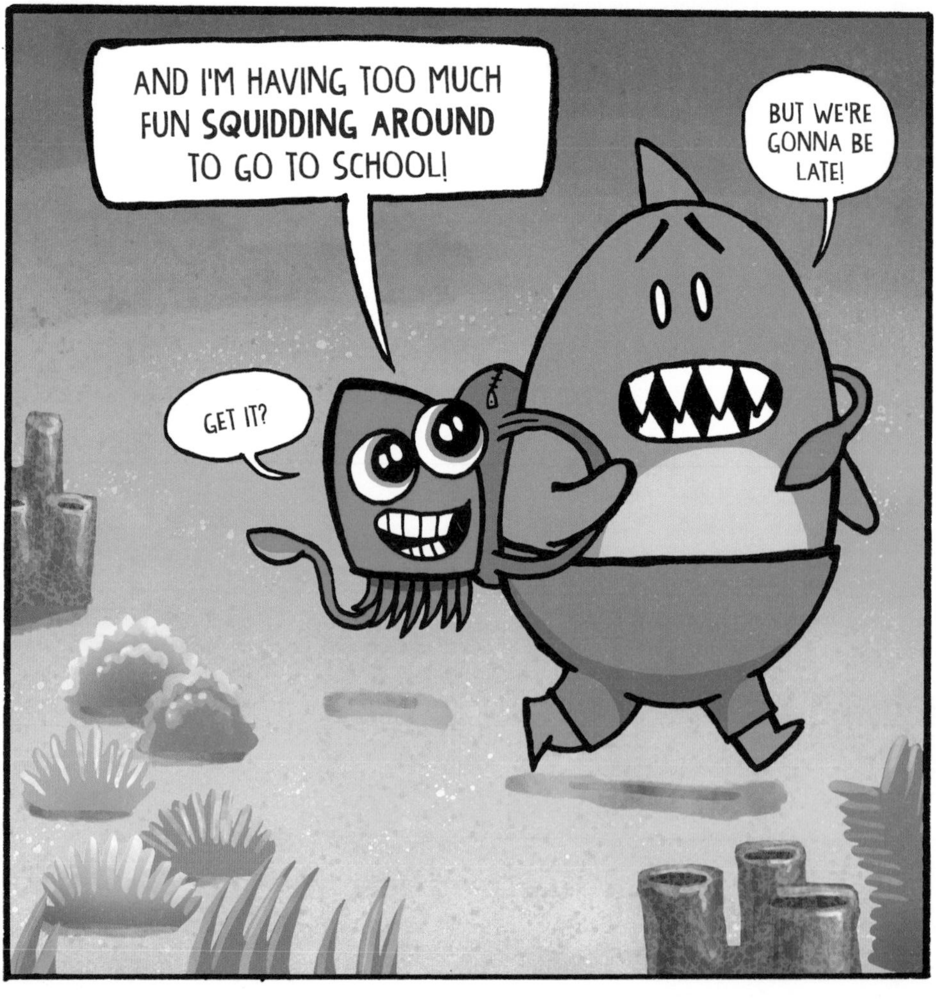
AND I'M HAVING TOO MUCH FUN SQUIDDING AROUND TO GO TO SCHOOL!
BUT WE'RE GONNA BE LATE!
GET IT?

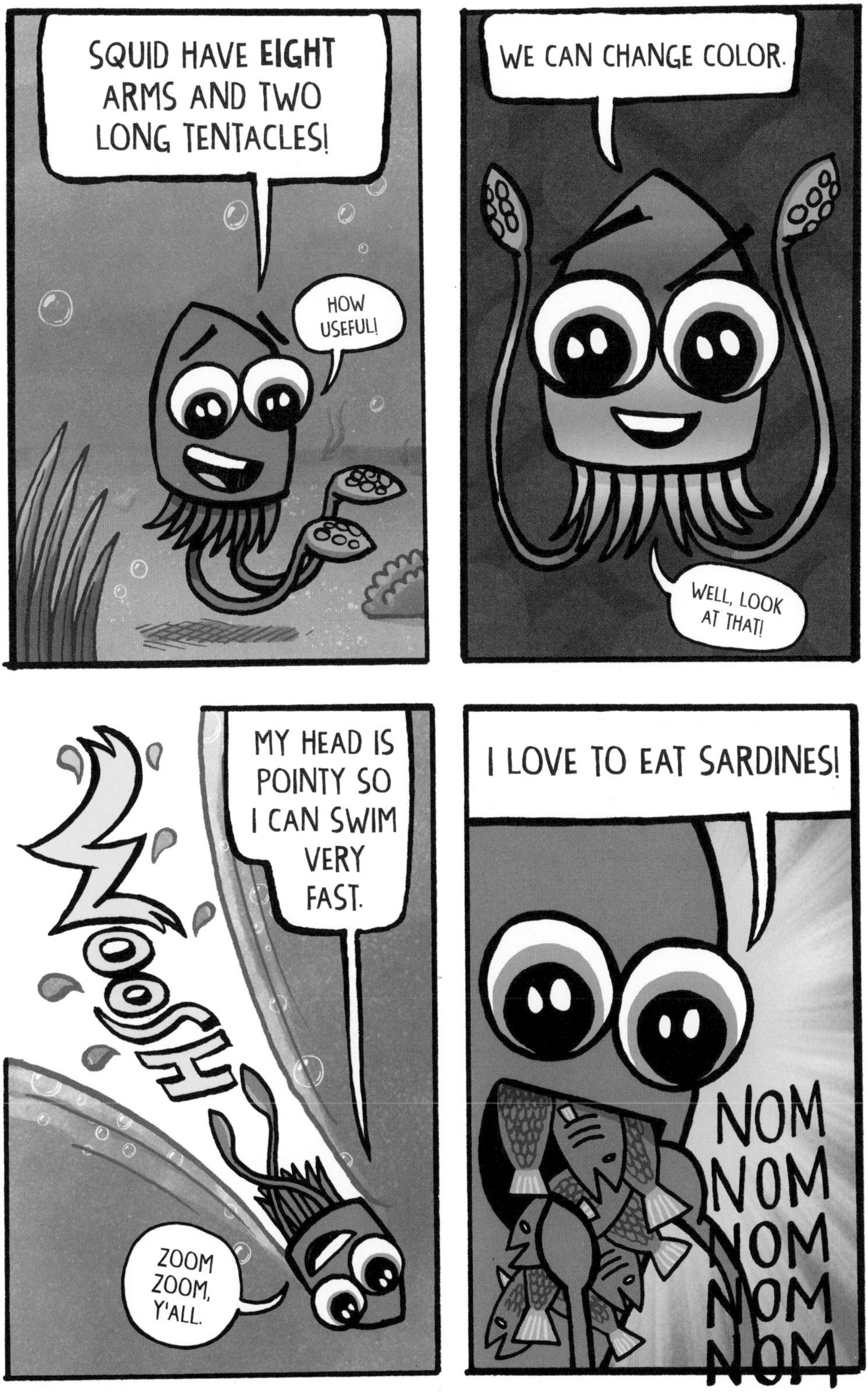
SQUID HAVE EIGHT ARMS AND TWO LONG TENTACLES!
HOW USEFUL!
WE CAN CHANGE COLOR.
WELL, LOOK AT THAT!
MY HEAD IS POINTY SO I CAN SWIM VERY FAST.
WOOSH
ZOOM ZOOM, Y'ALL.
I LOVE TO EAT SARDINES!
NOM NOM NOM NOM NOM

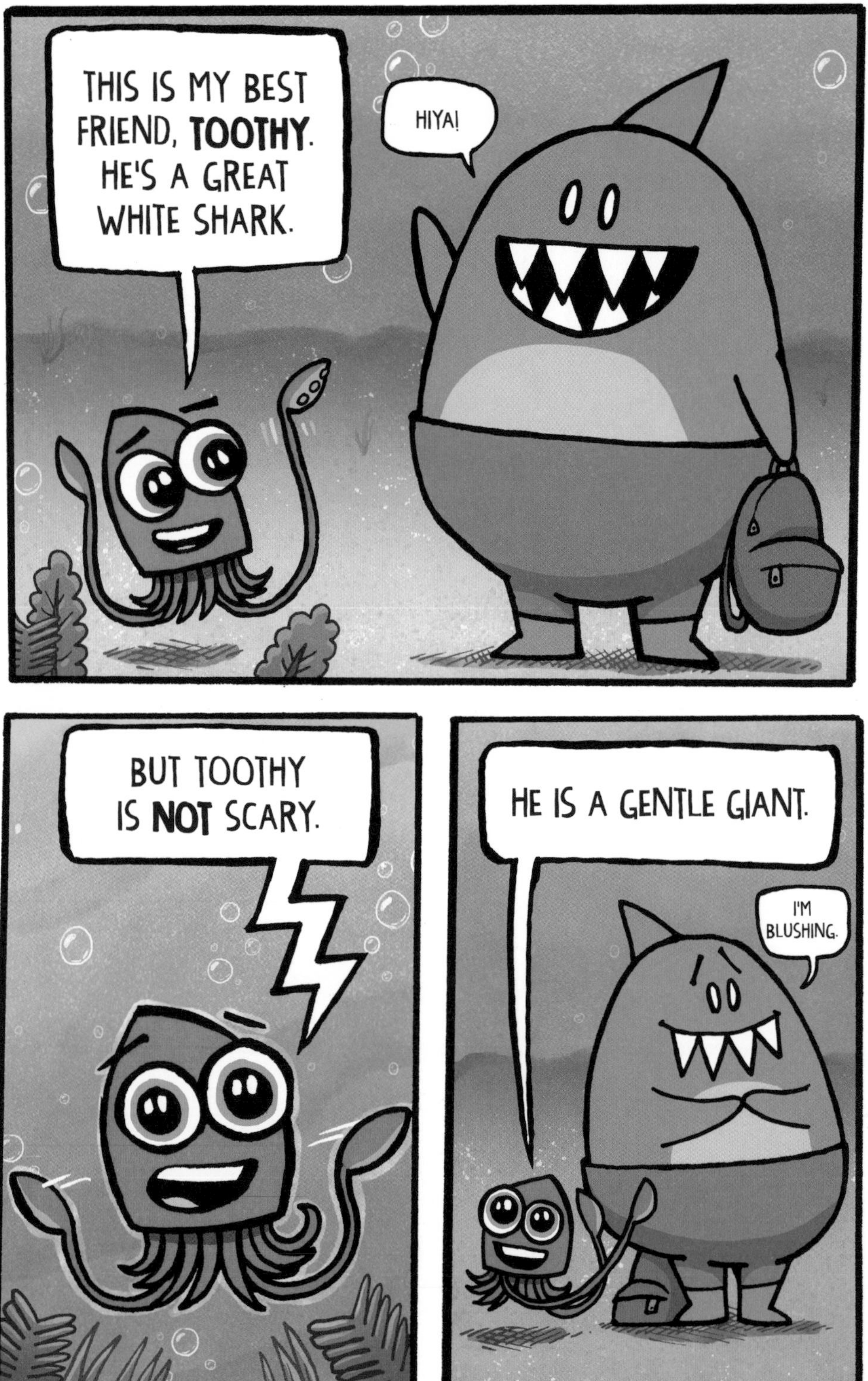
THIS IS MY BEST FRIEND, **TOOTHY**. HE'S A GREAT WHITE SHARK.
HIYA!
BUT TOOTHY IS **NOT** SCARY.
HE IS A GENTLE GIANT.
I'M BLUSHING.

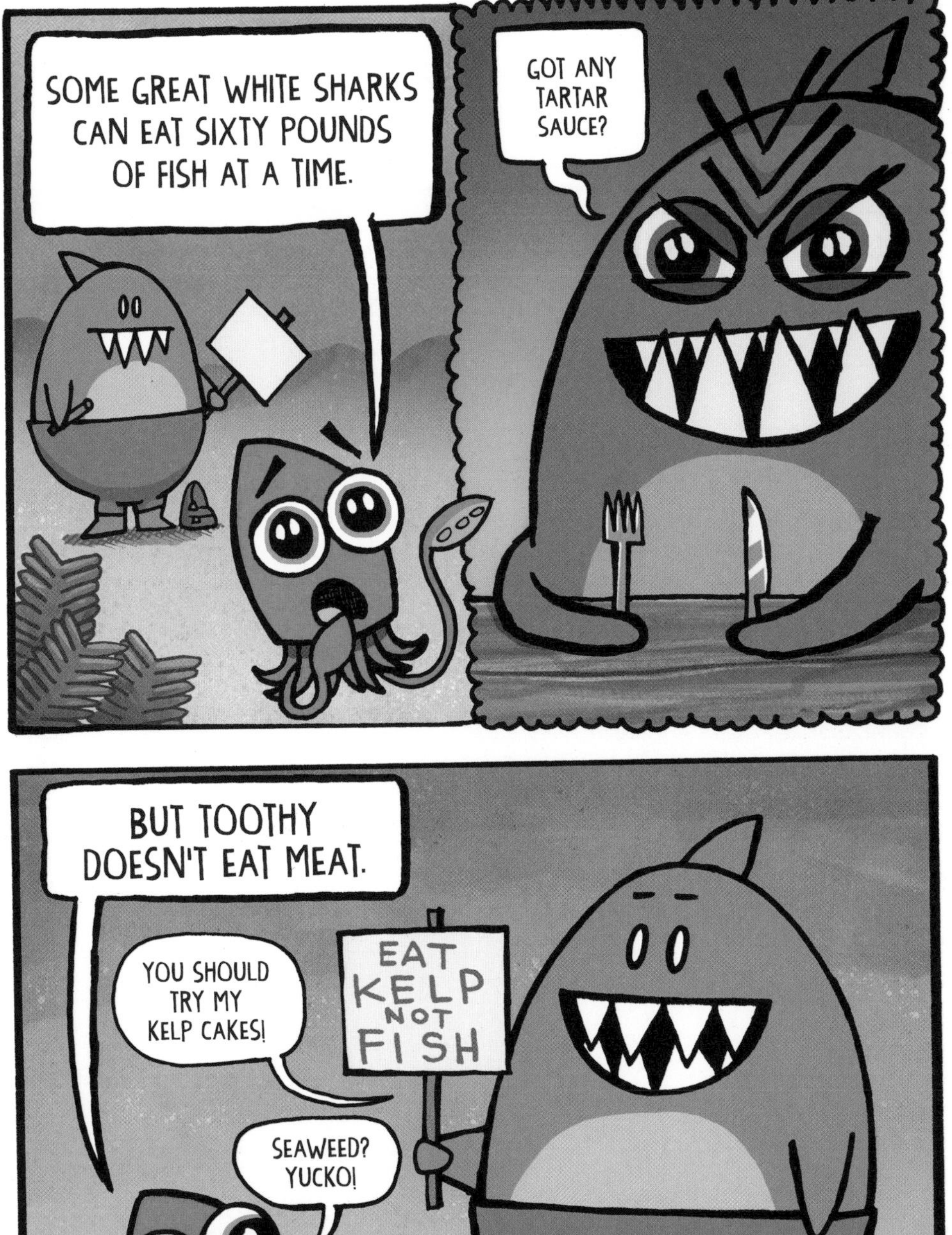
SOME GREAT WHITE SHARKS CAN EAT SIXTY POUNDS OF FISH AT A TIME.
GOT ANY TARTAR SAUCE?
BUT TOOTHY DOESN'T EAT MEAT.
YOU SHOULD TRY MY KELP CAKES!
EAT KELP NOT FISH
SEAWEED? YUCKO!

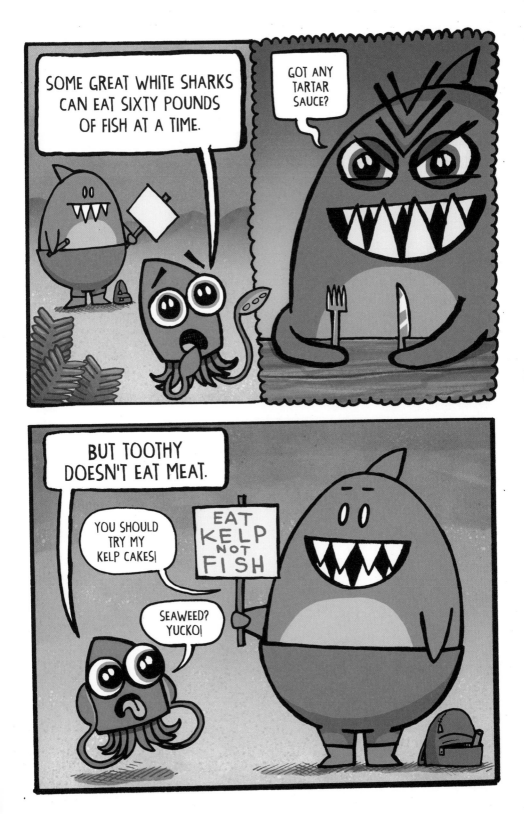

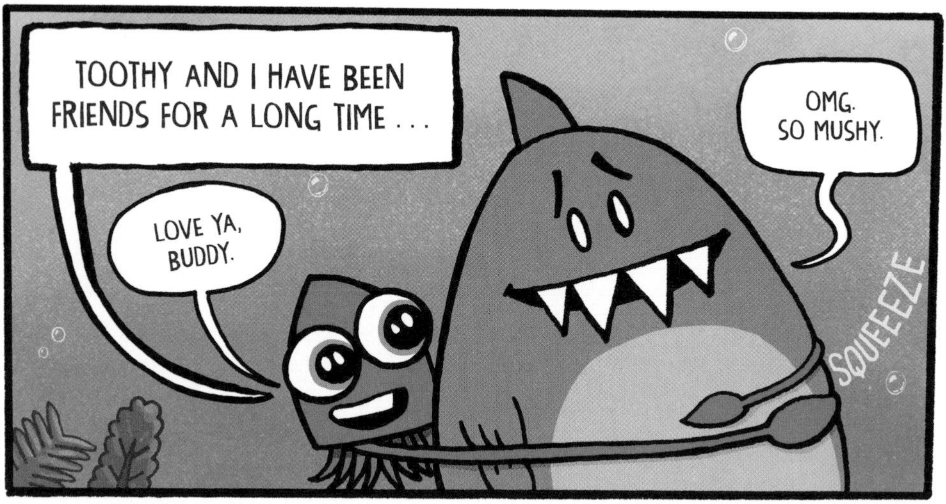
TOOTHY AND I HAVE BEEN FRIENDS FOR A LONG TIME . . .
LOVE YA, BUDDY.
OMG. SO MUSHY.
SQUEEEZE

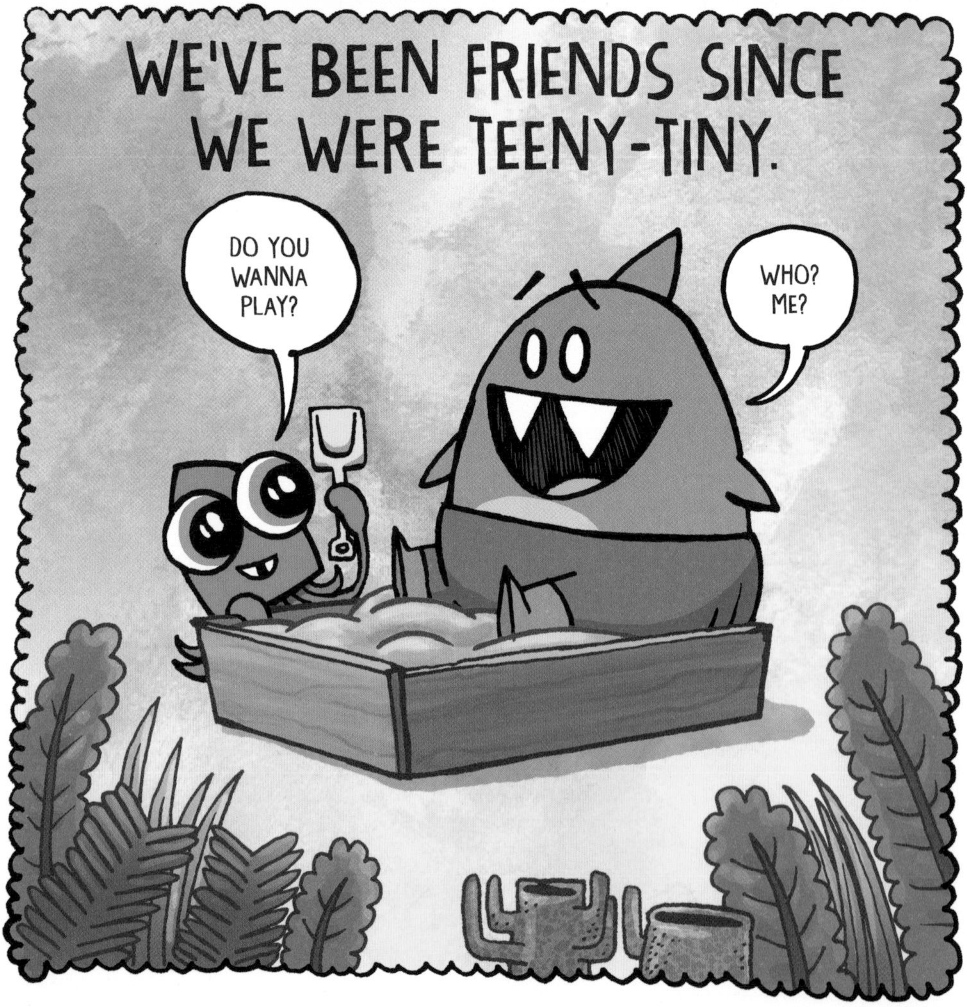
WE'VE BEEN FRIENDS SINCE WE WERE TEENY-TINY.
DO YOU WANNA PLAY?
WHO? ME?

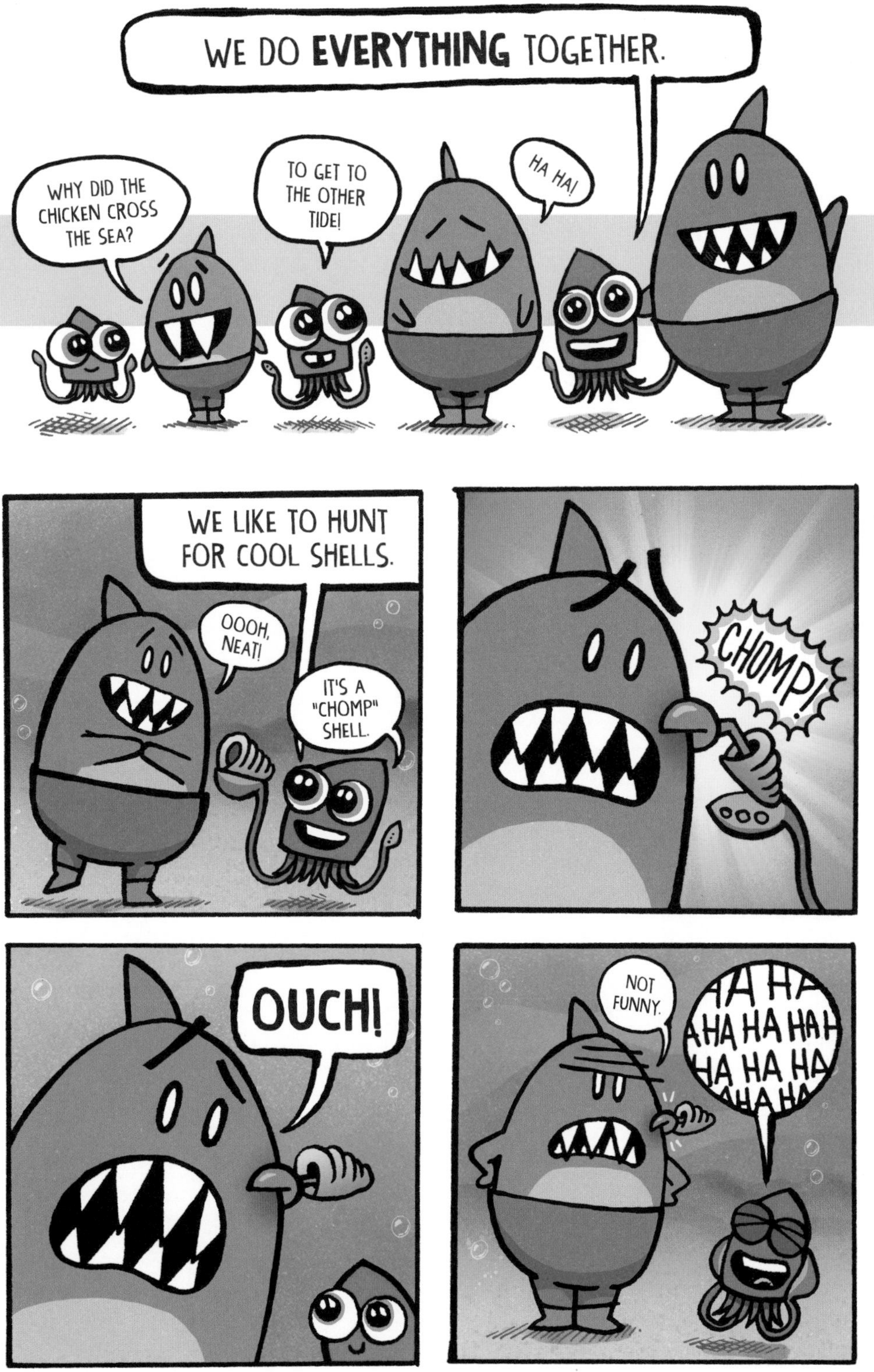
WE DO EVERYTHING TOGETHER.
WHY DID THE CHICKEN CROSS THE SEA?
TO GET TO THE OTHER TIDE!
HA HA!
WE LIKE TO HUNT FOR COOL SHELLS.
OOOH, NEAT!
IT'S A "CHOMP" SHELL.
CHOMP!
OUCH!
NOT FUNNY.
HA HA HA HA HA HA HA HA HA HA HA

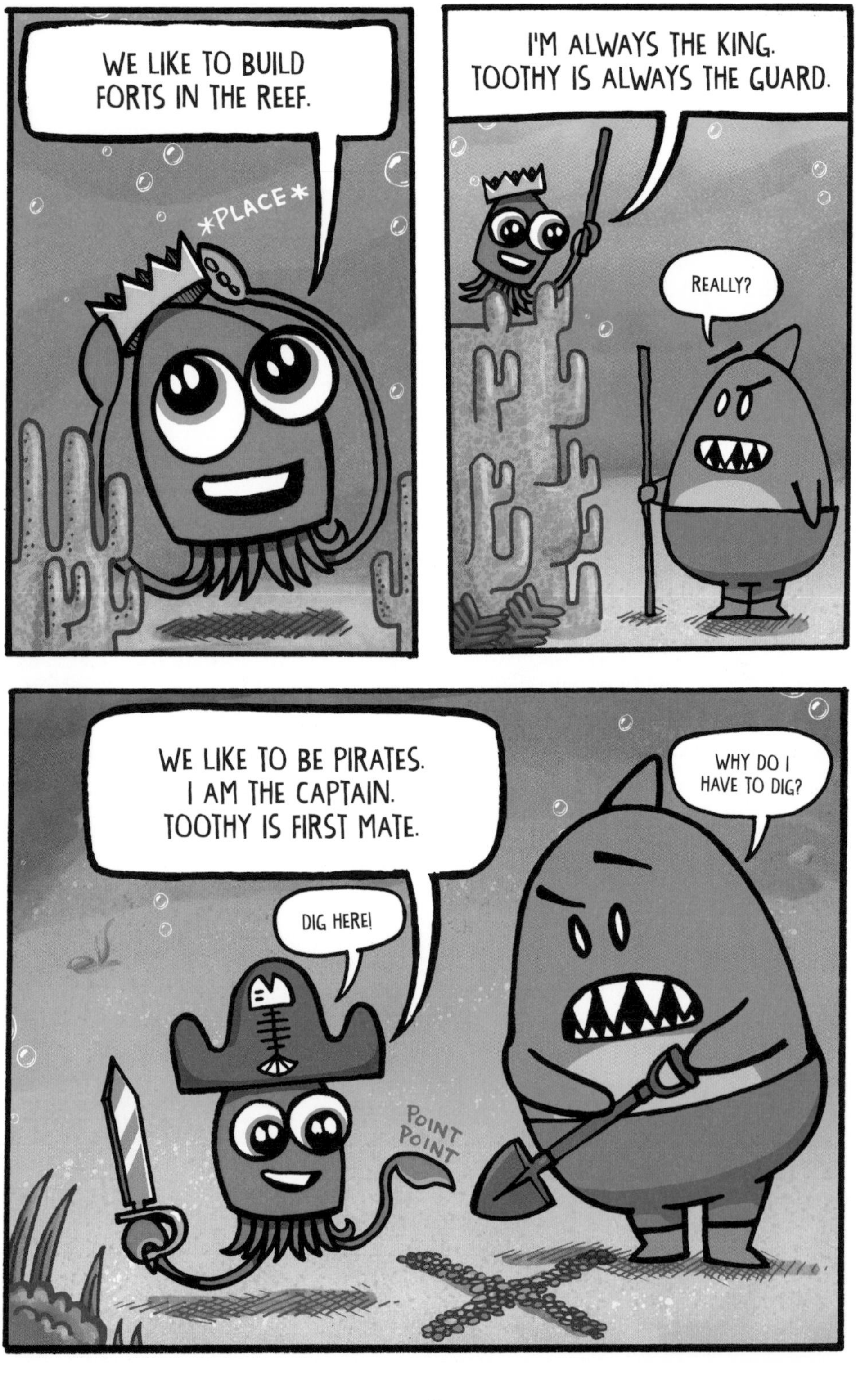
WE LIKE TO BUILD FORTS IN THE REEF.
PLACE
I'M ALWAYS THE KING. TOOTHY IS ALWAYS THE GUARD.
REALLY?
WE LIKE TO BE PIRATES. I AM THE CAPTAIN. TOOTHY IS FIRST MATE.
WHY DO I HAVE TO DIG?
DIG HERE!
POINT POINT

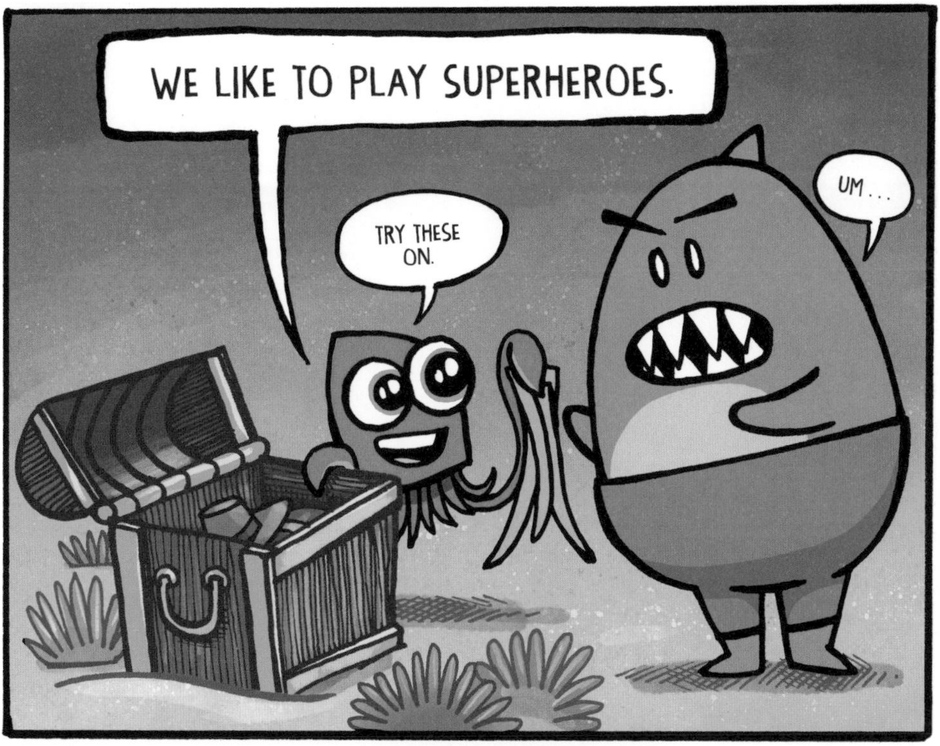
WE LIKE TO PLAY SUPERHEROES.
TRY THESE ON.
UM...

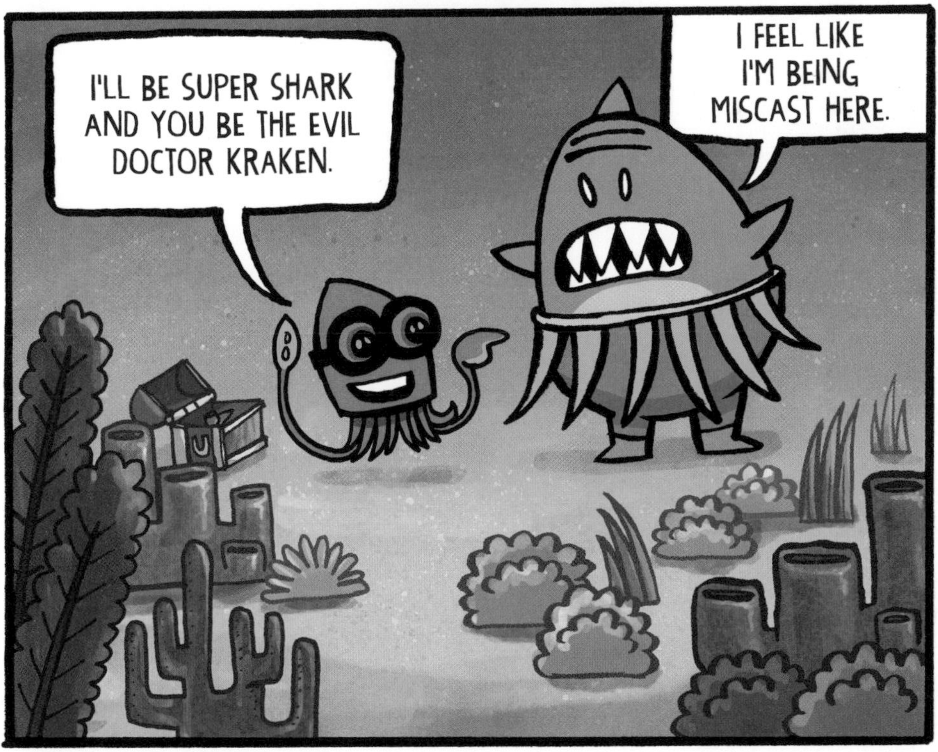
I'LL BE SUPER SHARK AND YOU BE THE EVIL DOCTOR KRAKEN.
I FEEL LIKE I'M BEING MISCAST HERE.

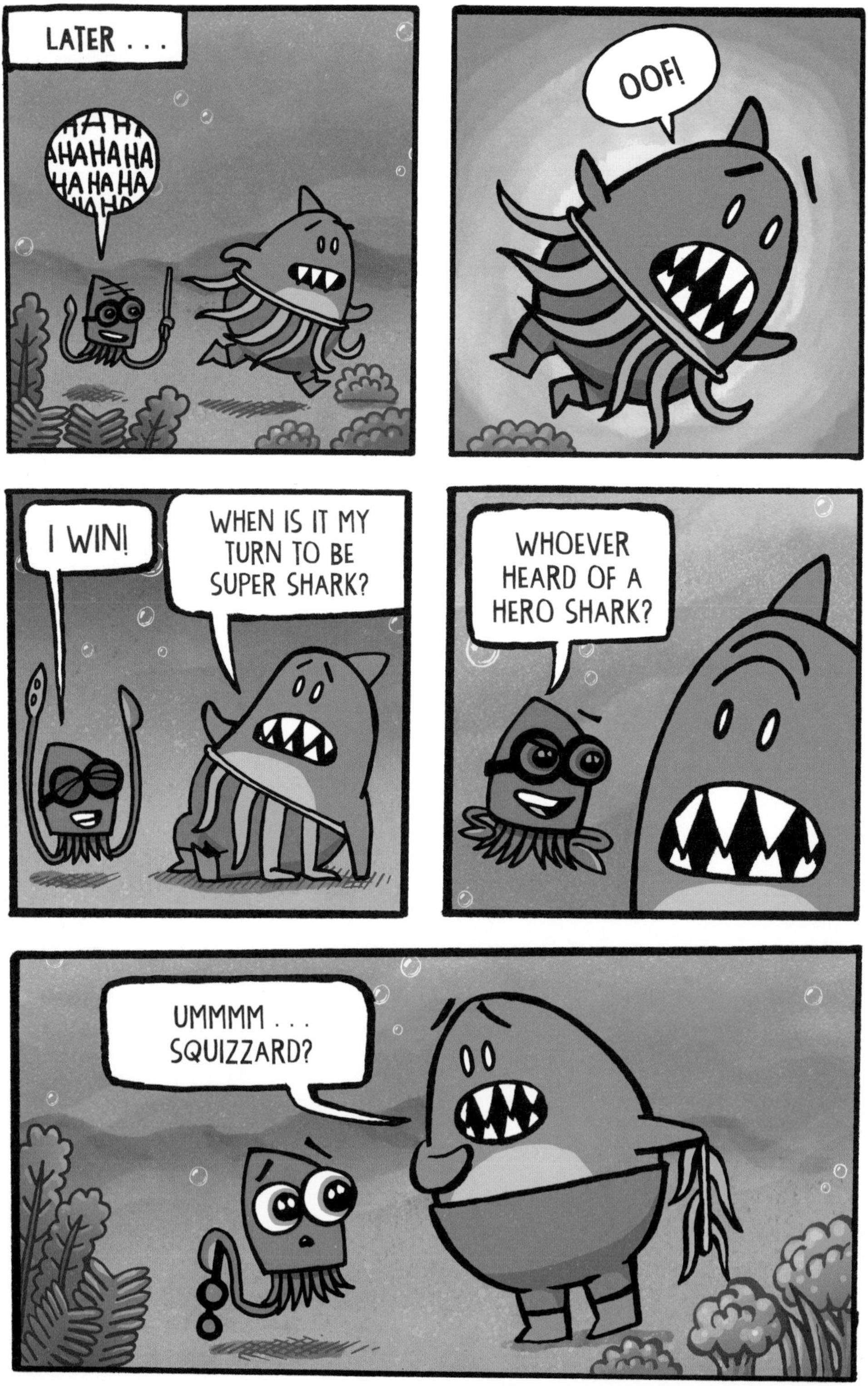
LATER . . .
HA HA HAHAHA HA HA HA
OOF!
I WIN!
WHEN IS IT MY TURN TO BE SUPER SHARK?
WHOEVER HEARD OF A HERO SHARK?
UMMMM . . . SQUIZZARD?

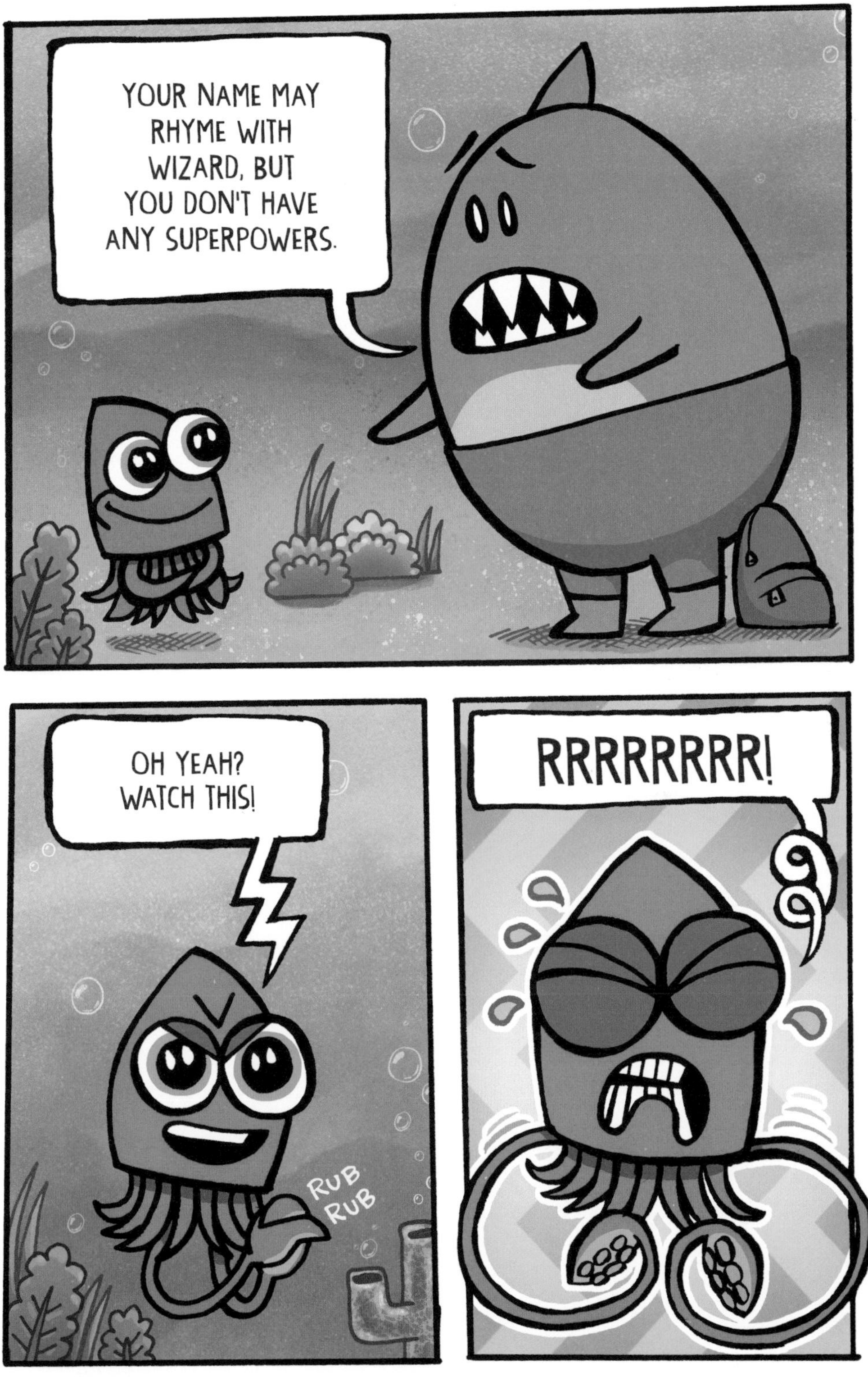
YOUR NAME MAY RHYME WITH WIZARD, BUT YOU DON'T HAVE ANY SUPERPOWERS.
OH YEAH? WATCH THIS!
RUB RUB
RRRRRRRR!

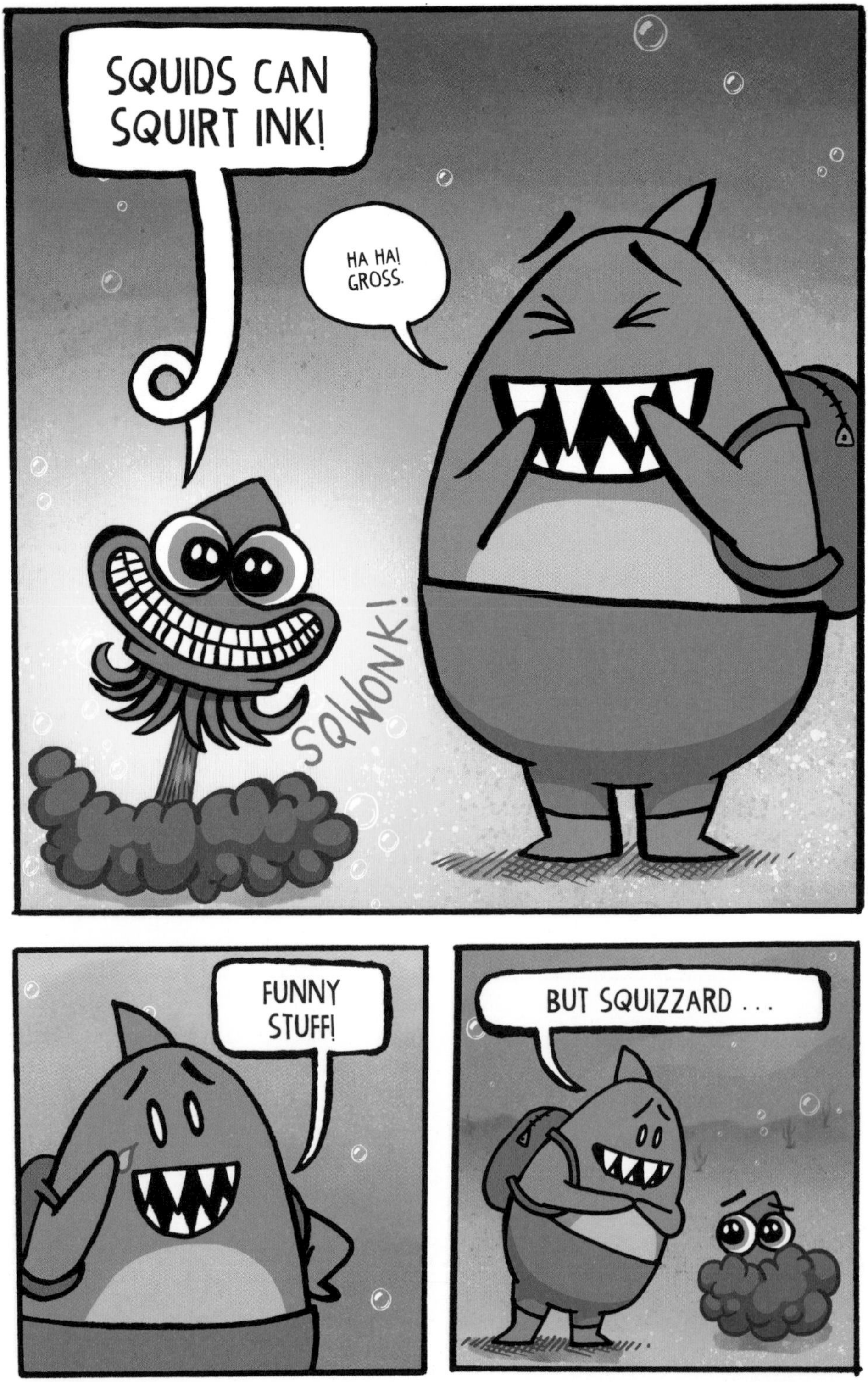
SQUIDS CAN SQUIRT INK!
HA HA! GROSS.
SQWONK!
FUNNY STUFF!
BUT SQUIZZARD . . .

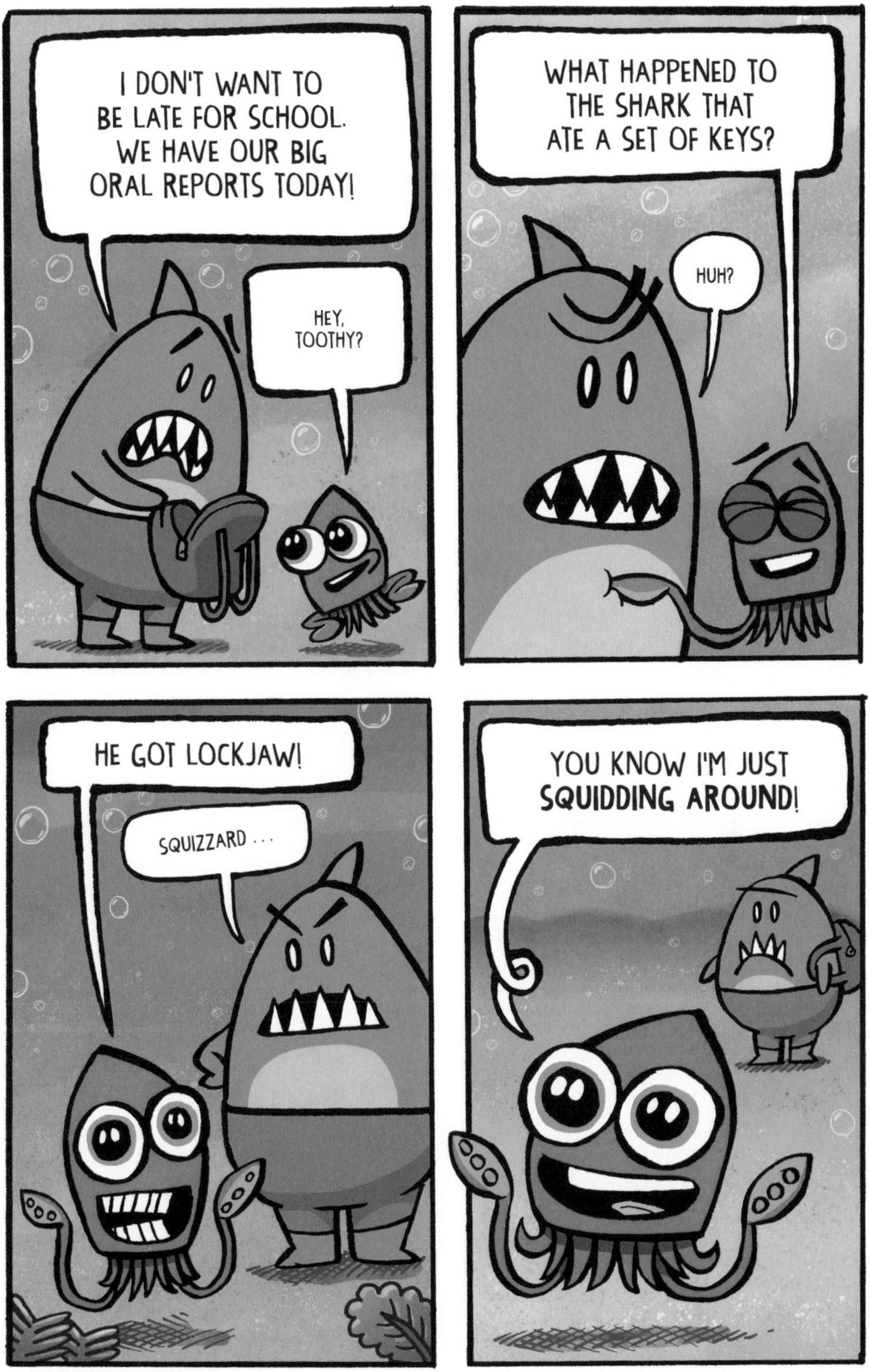
I DON'T WANT TO BE LATE FOR SCHOOL. WE HAVE OUR BIG ORAL REPORTS TODAY!
HEY, TOOTHY?
WHAT HAPPENED TO THE SHARK THAT ATE A SET OF KEYS?
HUH?
HE GOT LOCKJAW!
SQUIZZARD . . .
YOU KNOW I'M JUST **SQUIDDING AROUND!**

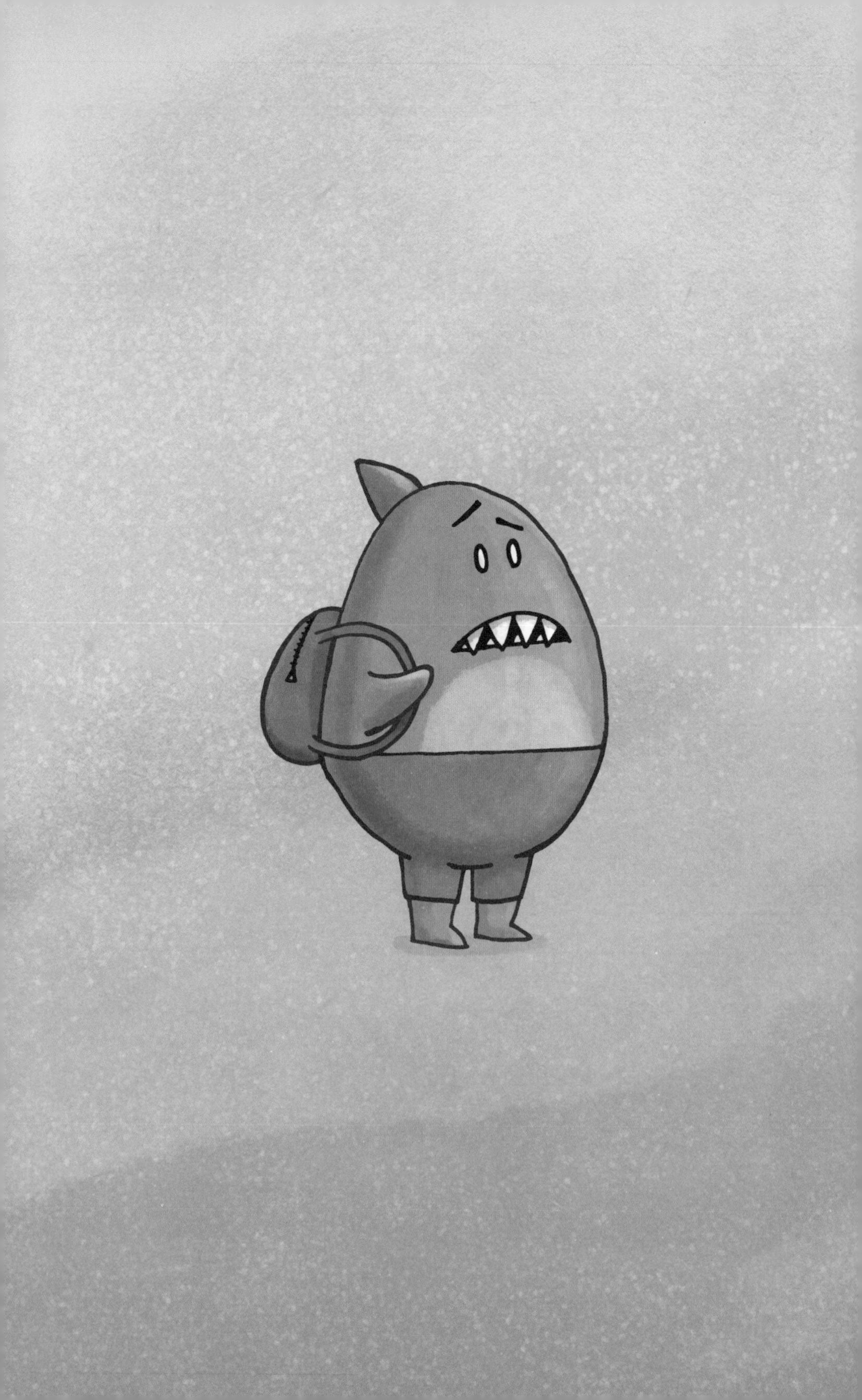

CHAPTER 2

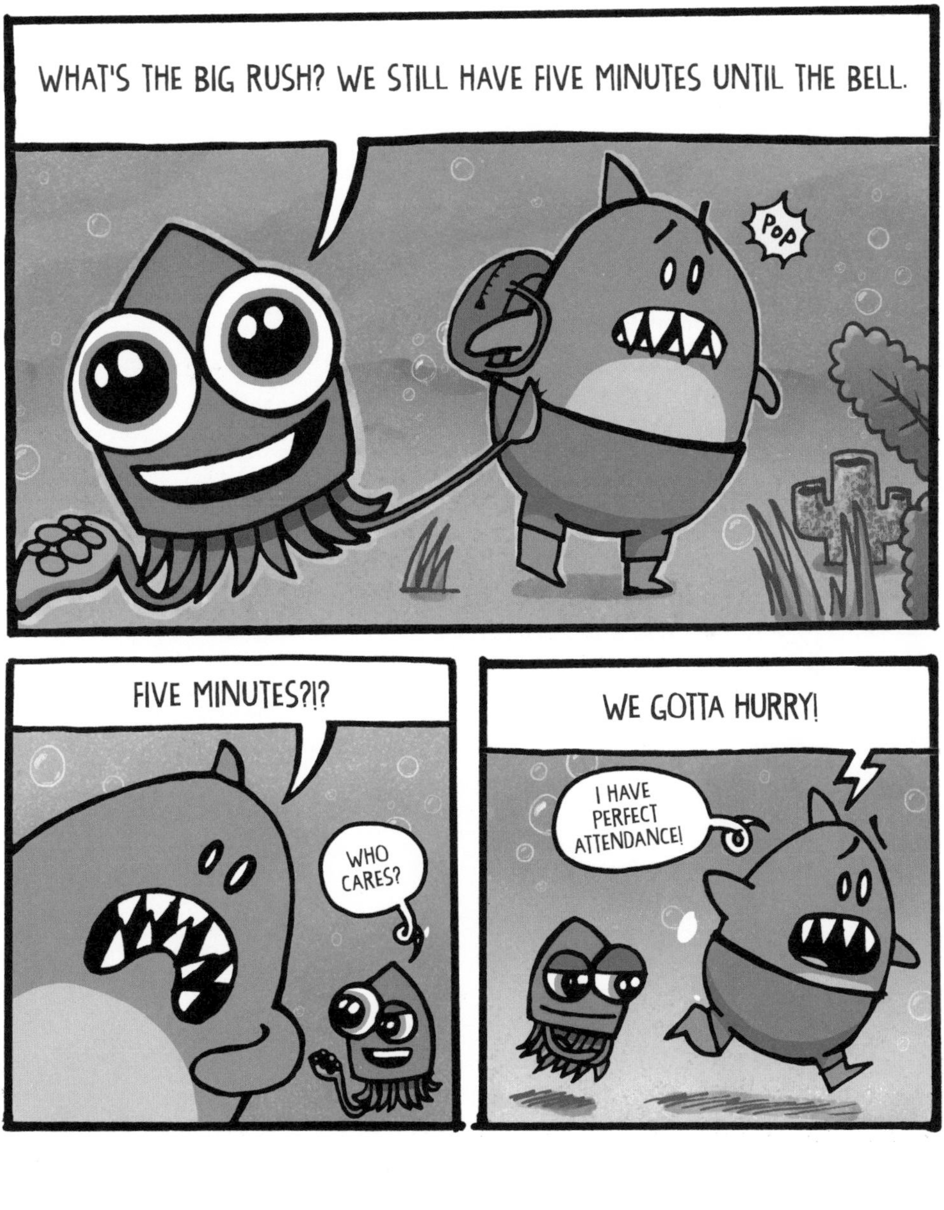
WHAT'S THE BIG RUSH? WE STILL HAVE FIVE MINUTES UNTIL THE BELL.
POP
FIVE MINUTES?!?
WHO CARES?
WE GOTTA HURRY!
I HAVE PERFECT ATTENDANCE!

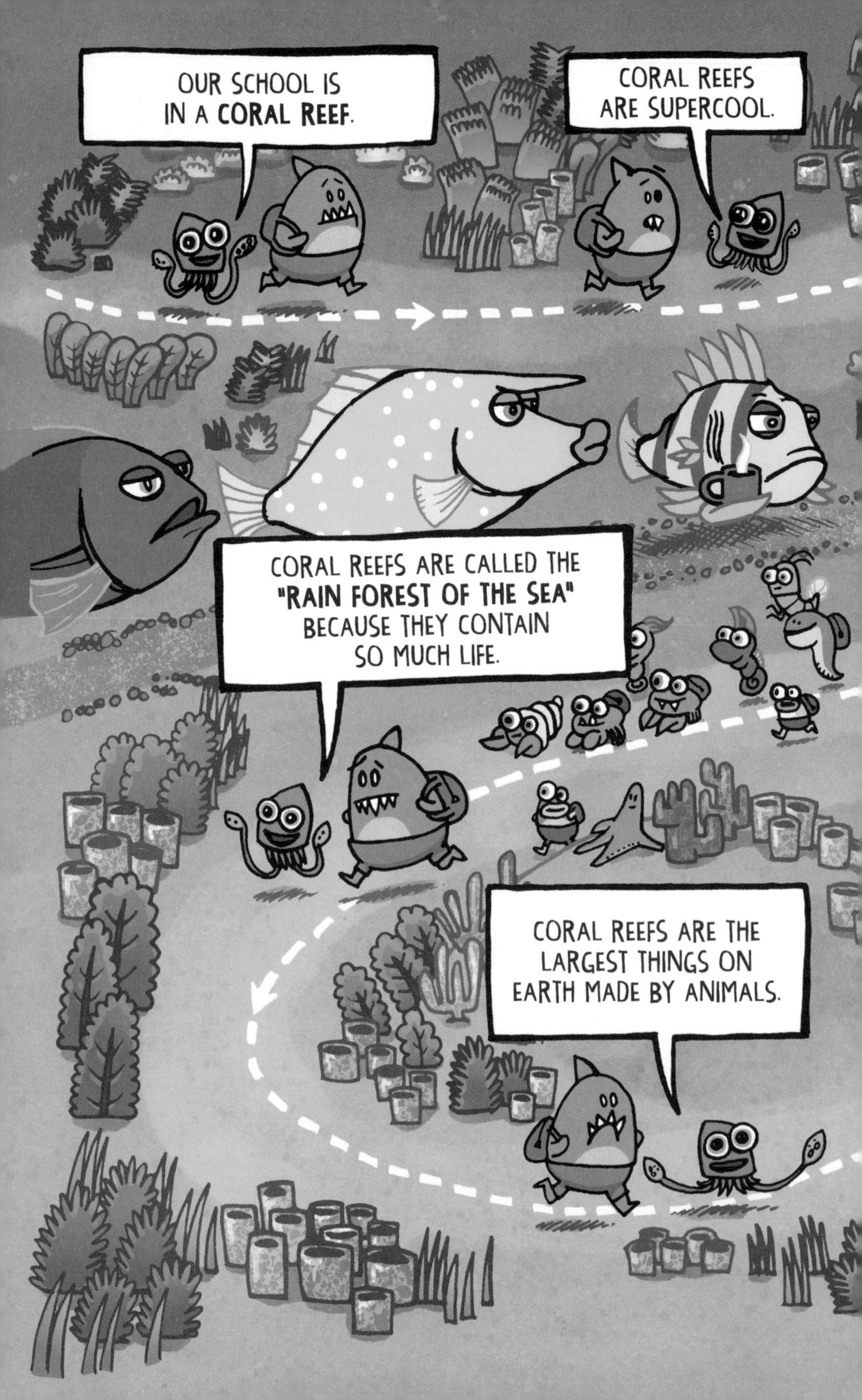
OUR SCHOOL IS IN A **CORAL REEF**.
CORAL REEFS ARE SUPERCOOL.
CORAL REEFS ARE CALLED THE **"RAIN FOREST OF THE SEA"** BECAUSE THEY CONTAIN SO MUCH LIFE.
CORAL REEFS ARE THE LARGEST THINGS ON EARTH MADE BY ANIMALS.

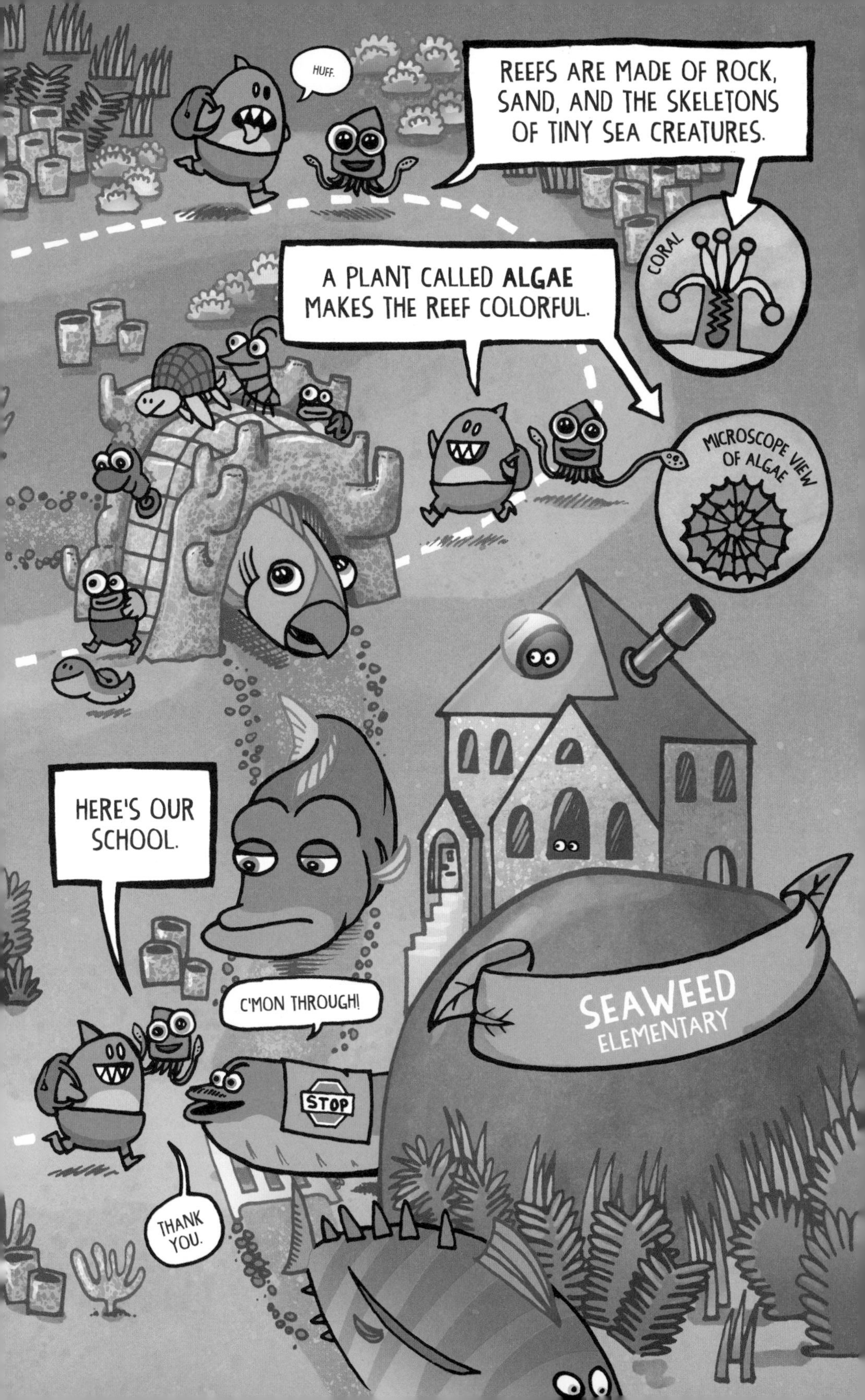
HUFF.
REEFS ARE MADE OF ROCK, SAND, AND THE SKELETONS OF TINY SEA CREATURES.
CORAL
A PLANT CALLED ALGAE MAKES THE REEF COLORFUL.
MICROSCOPE VIEW OF ALGAE
HERE'S OUR SCHOOL.
C'MON THROUGH!
STOP
SEAWEED ELEMENTARY
THANK YOU.

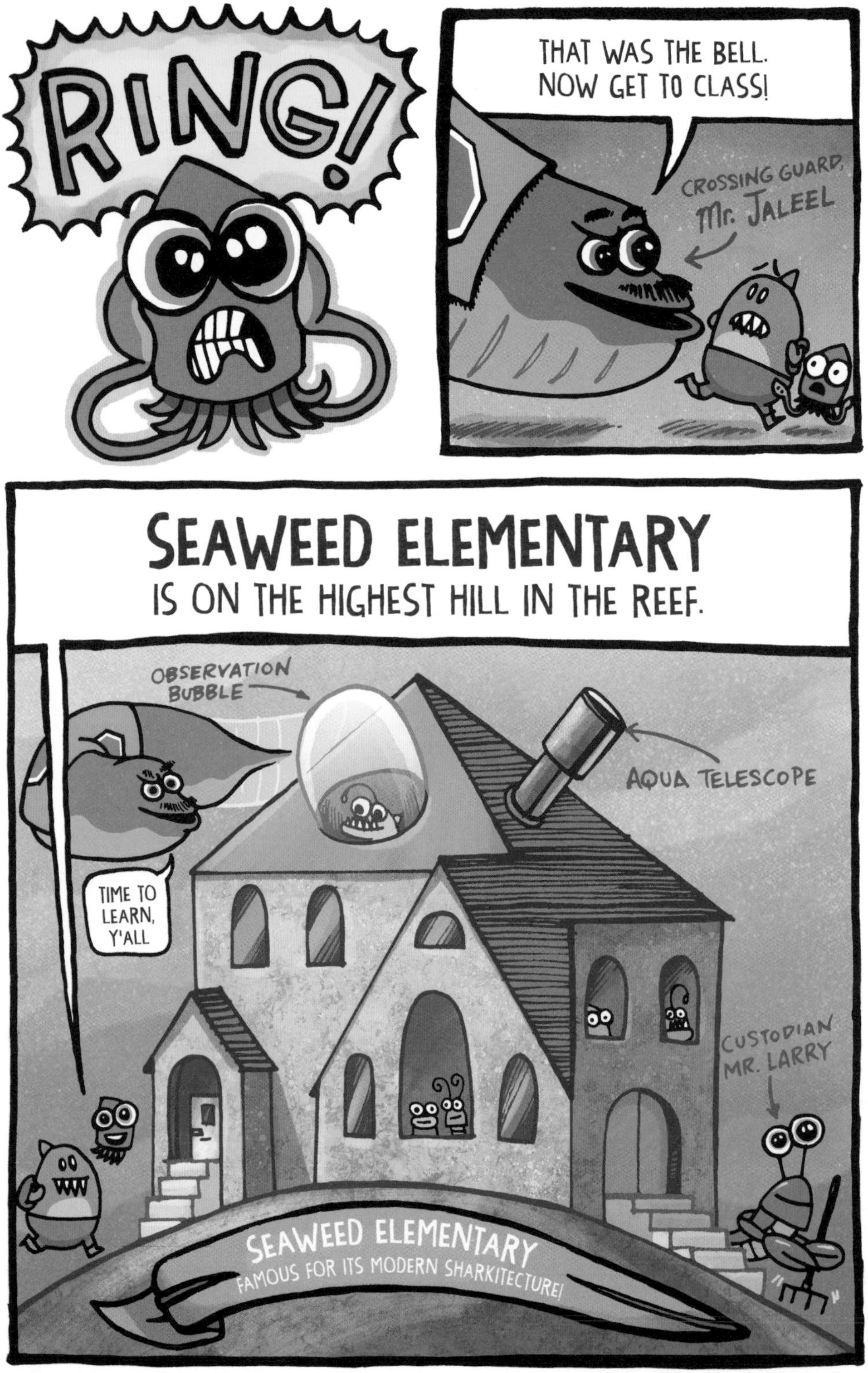
RING!
THAT WAS THE BELL. NOW GET TO CLASS!
CROSSING GUARD, Mr. JALEEL
SEAWEED ELEMENTARY
IS ON THE HIGHEST HILL IN THE REEF.
OBSERVATION BUBBLE
AQUA TELESCOPE
TIME TO LEARN, Y'ALL
CUSTODIAN MR. LARRY
SEAWEED ELEMENTARY
FAMOUS FOR ITS MODERN SHARKITECTURE!

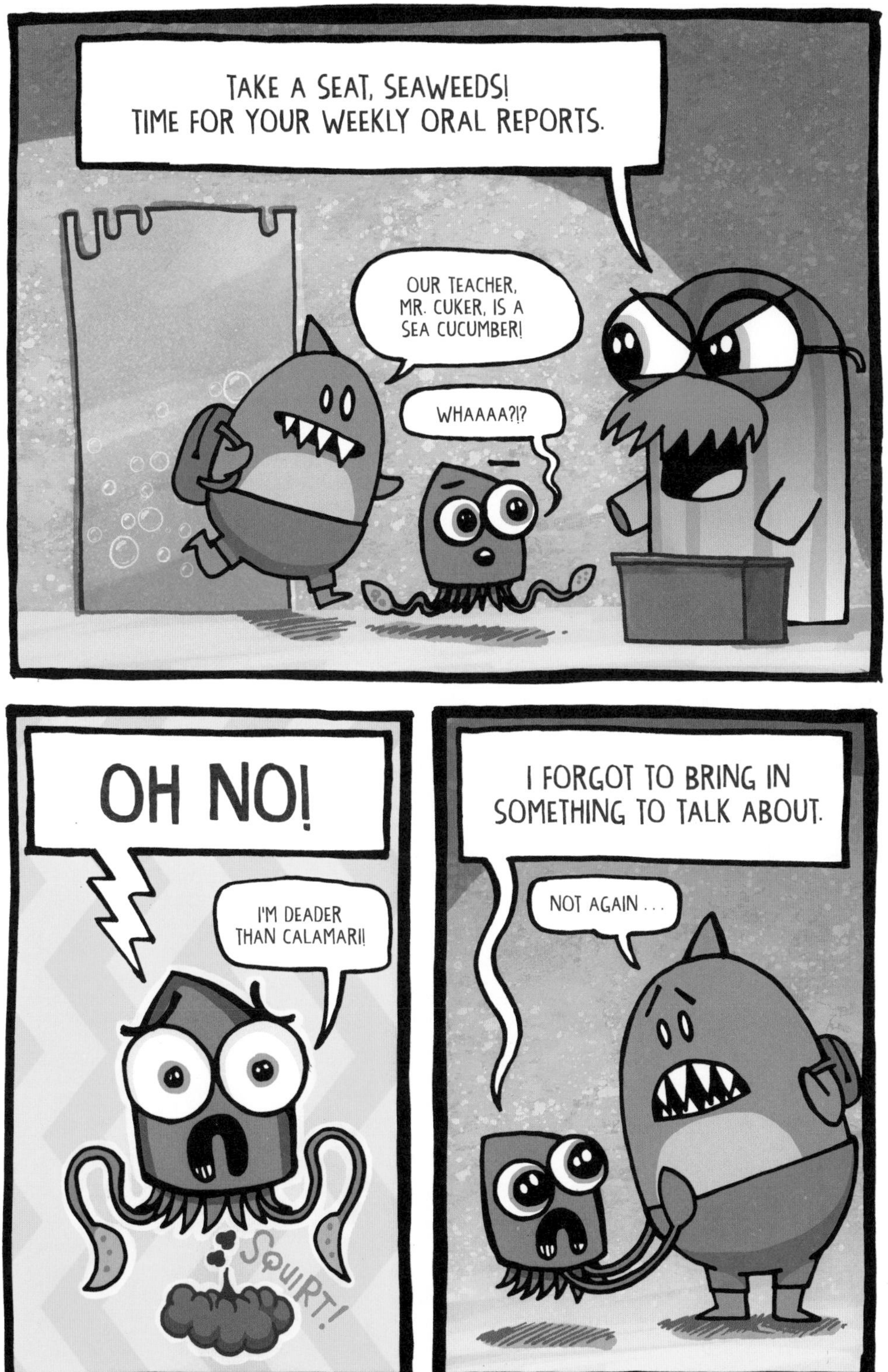
TAKE A SEAT, SEAWEEDS! TIME FOR YOUR WEEKLY ORAL REPORTS.
OUR TEACHER, MR. CUKER, IS A SEA CUCUMBER!
WHAAAA?!?
OH NO!
I'M DEADER THAN CALAMARI!
SQUIRT!
I FORGOT TO BRING IN SOMETHING TO TALK ABOUT.
NOT AGAIN . . .

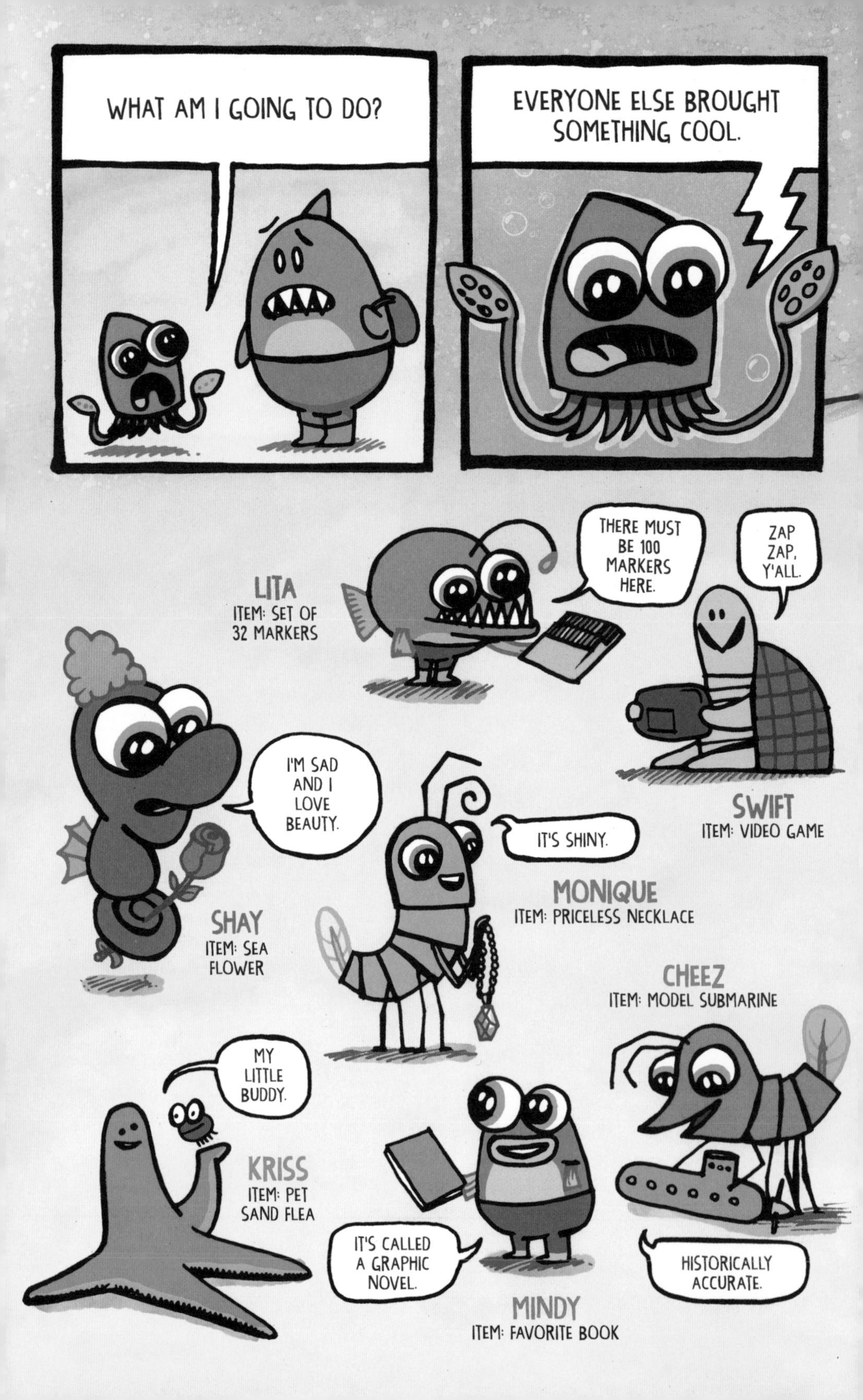
WHAT AM I GOING TO DO?
EVERYONE ELSE BROUGHT SOMETHING COOL.
LITA
ITEM: SET OF 32 MARKERS
THERE MUST BE 100 MARKERS HERE.
ZAP ZAP, Y'ALL.
SWIFT
ITEM: VIDEO GAME
I'M SAD AND I LOVE BEAUTY.
SHAY
ITEM: SEA FLOWER
IT'S SHINY.
MONIQUE
ITEM: PRICELESS NECKLACE
CHEEZ
ITEM: MODEL SUBMARINE
MY LITTLE BUDDY.
KRISS
ITEM: PET SAND FLEA
IT'S CALLED A GRAPHIC NOVEL.
MINDY
ITEM: FAVORITE BOOK
HISTORICALLY ACCURATE.

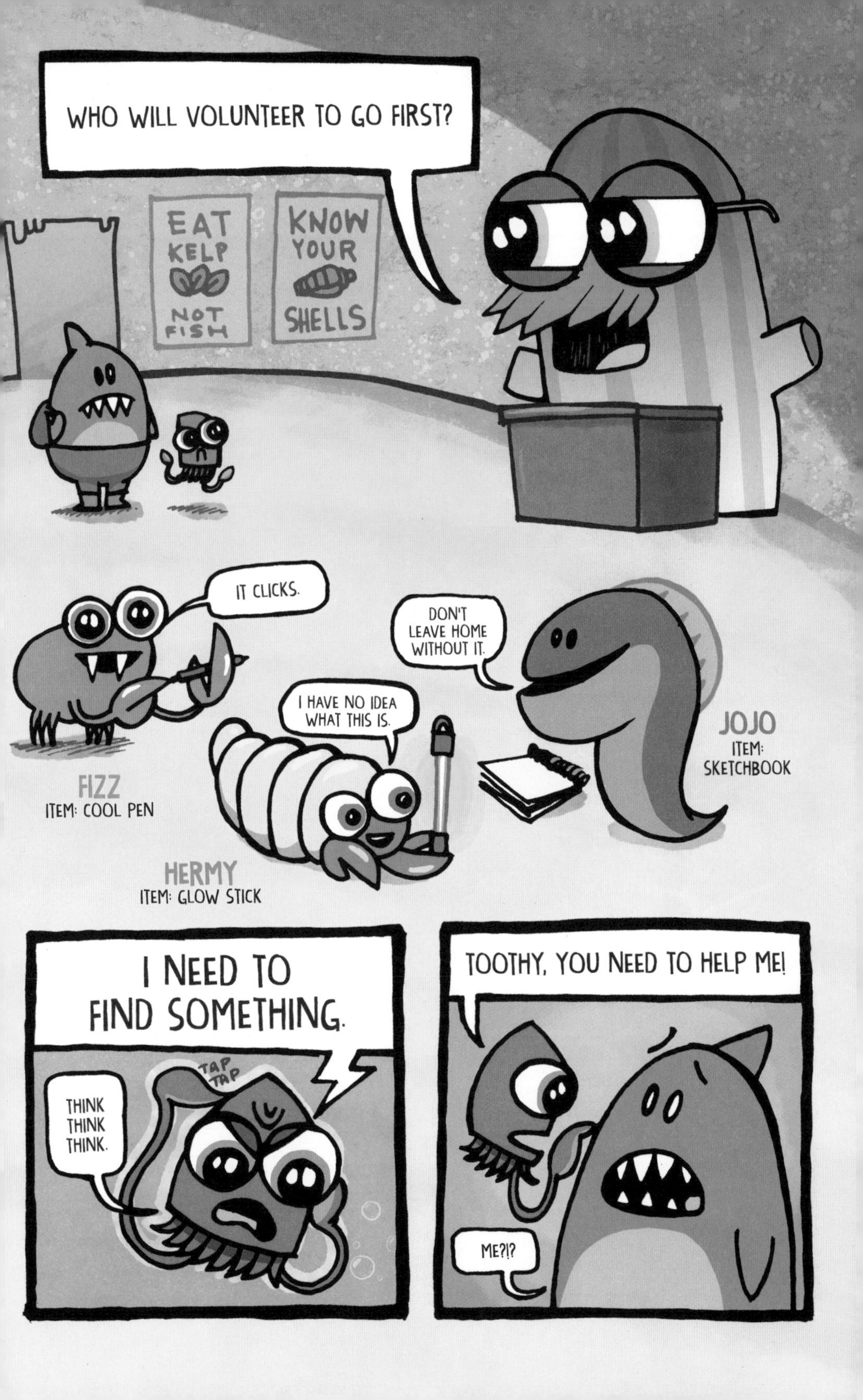
WHO WILL VOLUNTEER TO GO FIRST?
EAT KELP NOT FISH
KNOW YOUR SHELLS
IT CLICKS.
DON'T LEAVE HOME WITHOUT IT.
I HAVE NO IDEA WHAT THIS IS.
JOJO
ITEM: SKETCHBOOK
FIZZ
ITEM: COOL PEN
HERMY
ITEM: GLOW STICK
I NEED TO FIND SOMETHING.
TAP TAP
THINK THINK THINK.
TOOTHY, YOU NEED TO HELP ME!
ME?!?

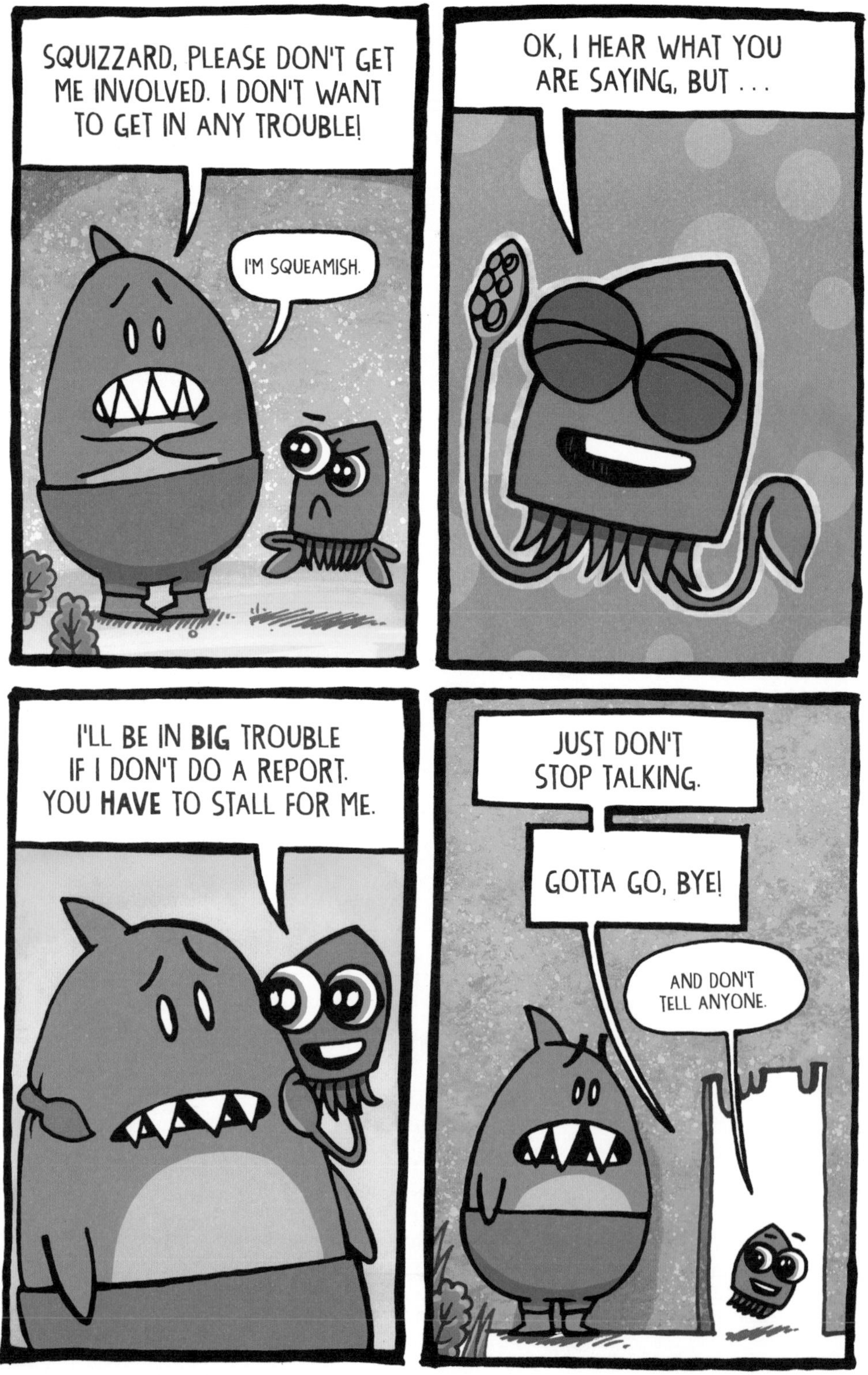
SQUIZZARD, PLEASE DON'T GET ME INVOLVED. I DON'T WANT TO GET IN ANY TROUBLE!
I'M SQUEAMISH.
OK, I HEAR WHAT YOU ARE SAYING, BUT . . .
I'LL BE IN **BIG** TROUBLE IF I DON'T DO A REPORT. YOU **HAVE** TO STALL FOR ME.
JUST DON'T STOP TALKING.
GOTTA GO, BYE!
AND DON'T TELL ANYONE.

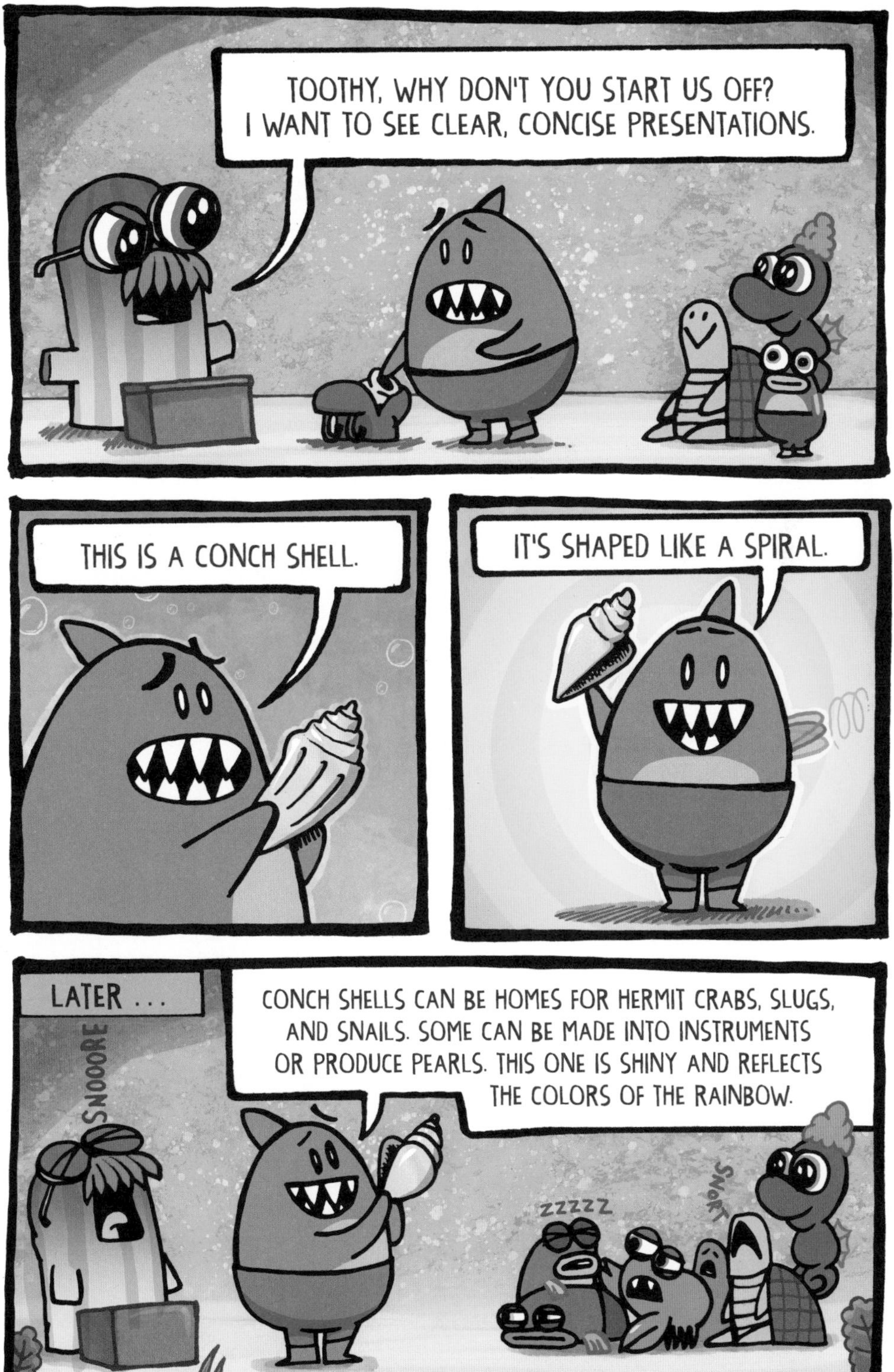
TOOTHY, WHY DON'T YOU START US OFF? I WANT TO SEE CLEAR, CONCISE PRESENTATIONS.
THIS IS A CONCH SHELL.
IT'S SHAPED LIKE A SPIRAL.
LATER . . .
SNOOORE
CONCH SHELLS CAN BE HOMES FOR HERMIT CRABS, SLUGS, AND SNAILS. SOME CAN BE MADE INTO INSTRUMENTS OR PRODUCE PEARLS. THIS ONE IS SHINY AND REFLECTS THE COLORS OF THE RAINBOW.
ZZZZZ
SNORT

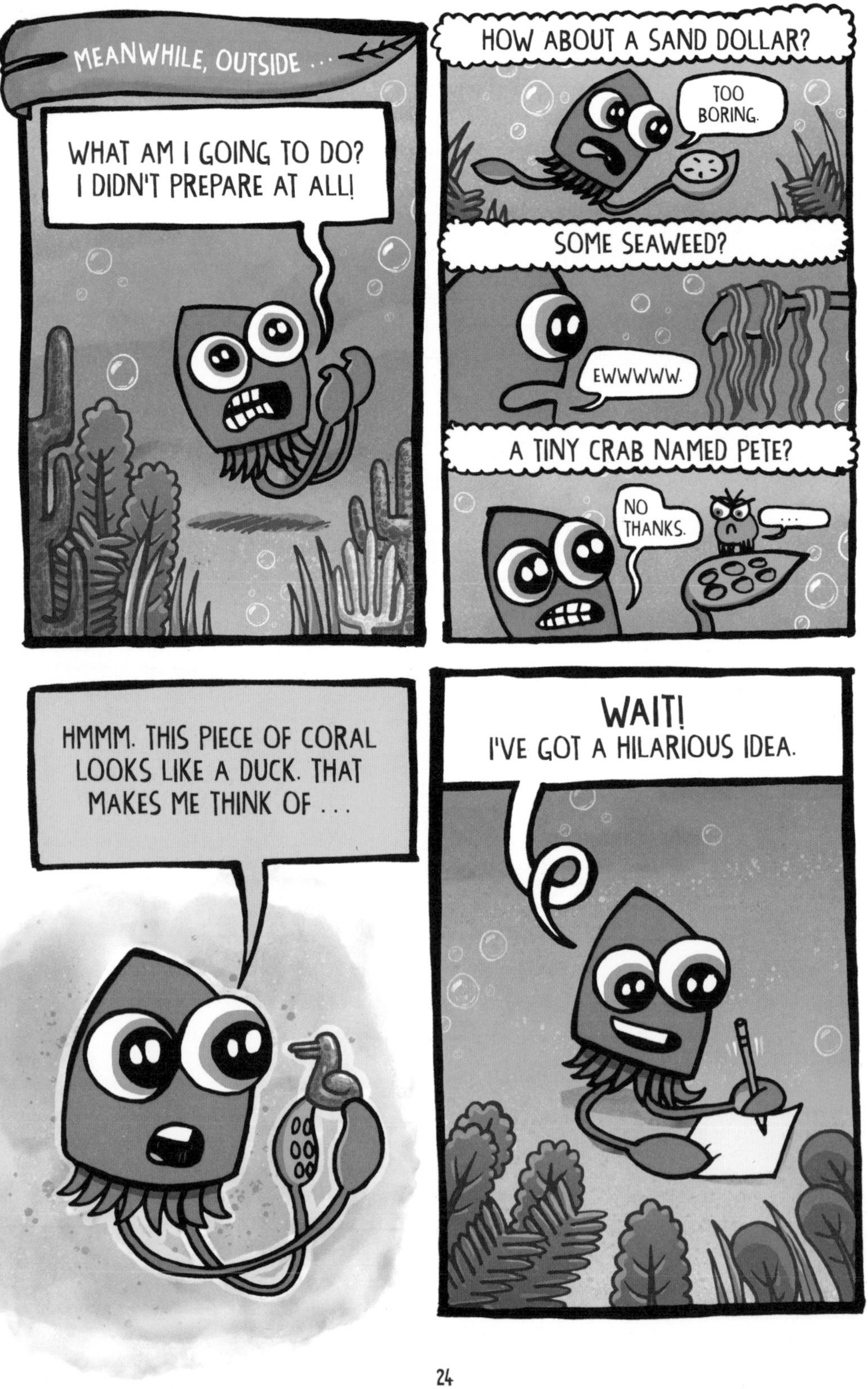
MEANWHILE, OUTSIDE . . .
WHAT AM I GOING TO DO? I DIDN'T PREPARE AT ALL!
HOW ABOUT A SAND DOLLAR?
TOO BORING.
SOME SEAWEED?
EWWWWW.
A TINY CRAB NAMED PETE?
NO THANKS.
. . .
HMMM. THIS PIECE OF CORAL LOOKS LIKE A DUCK. THAT MAKES ME THINK OF . . .
WAIT!
I'VE GOT A HILARIOUS IDEA.

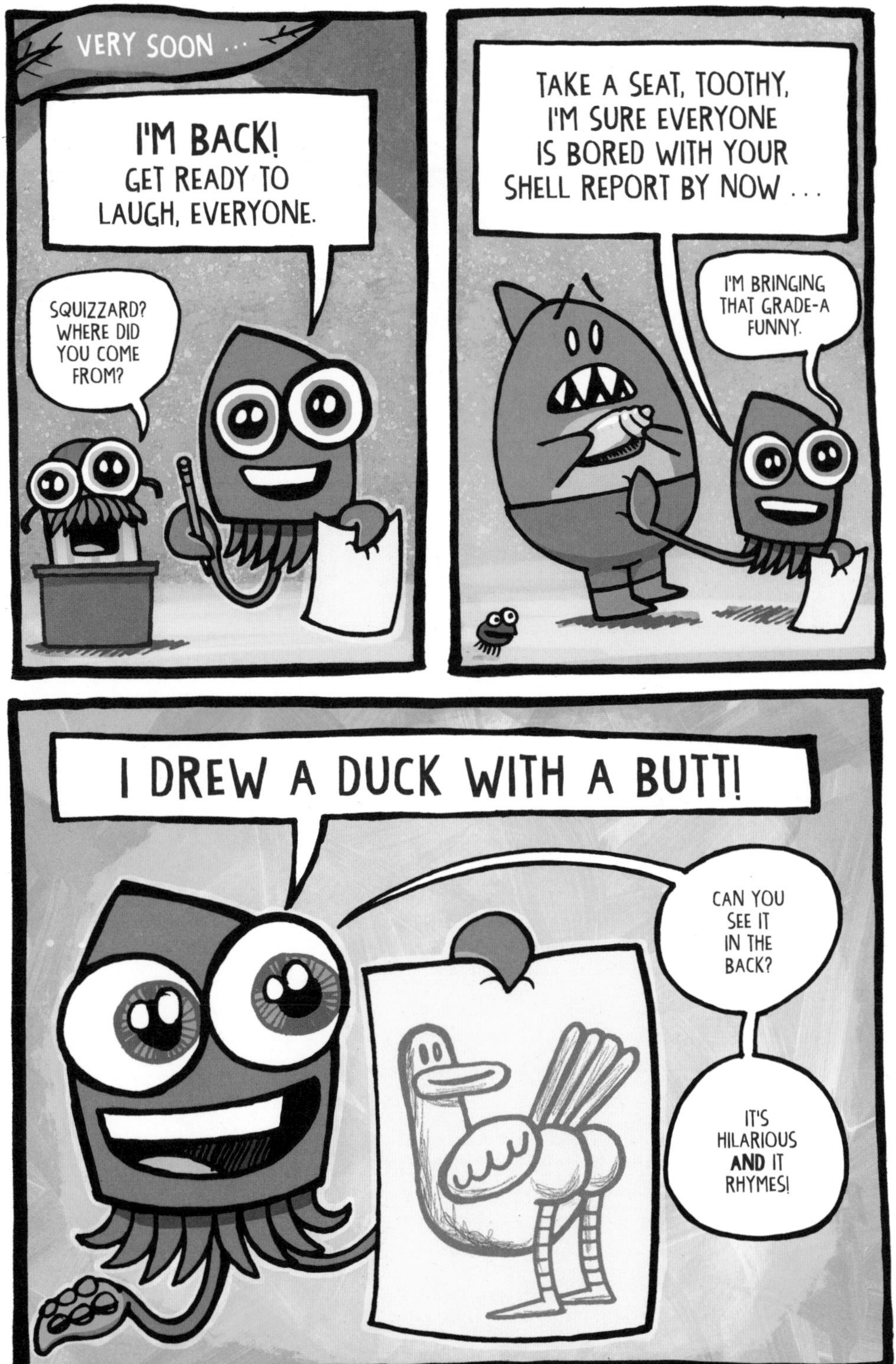
VERY SOON . . .
I'M BACK! GET READY TO LAUGH, EVERYONE.
SQUIZZARD? WHERE DID YOU COME FROM?
TAKE A SEAT, TOOTHY, I'M SURE EVERYONE IS BORED WITH YOUR SHELL REPORT BY NOW . . .
I'M BRINGING THAT GRADE-A FUNNY.
I DREW A DUCK WITH A BUTT!
CAN YOU SEE IT IN THE BACK?
IT'S HILARIOUS **AND** IT RHYMES!

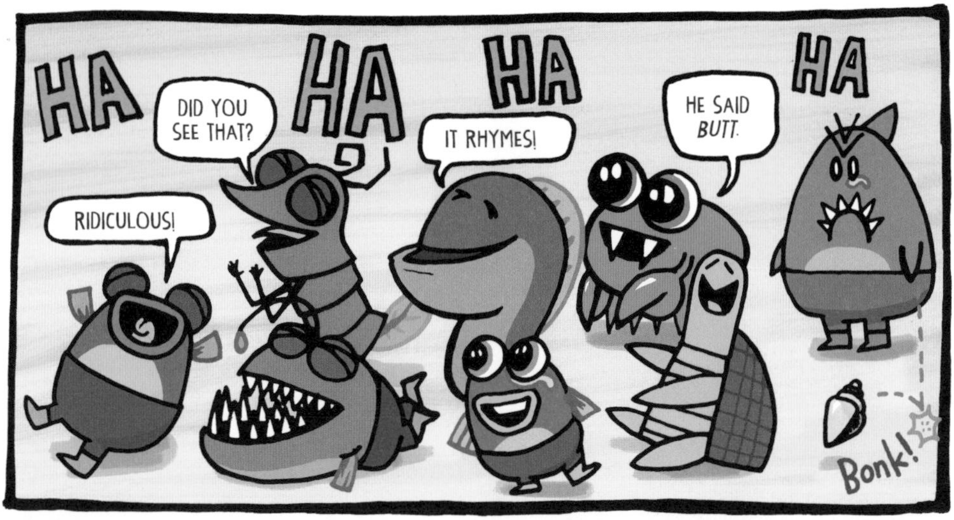
HA
RIDICULOUS!
DID YOU SEE THAT?
HA
HA
IT RHYMES!
HE SAID *BUTT*.
HA
Bonk!

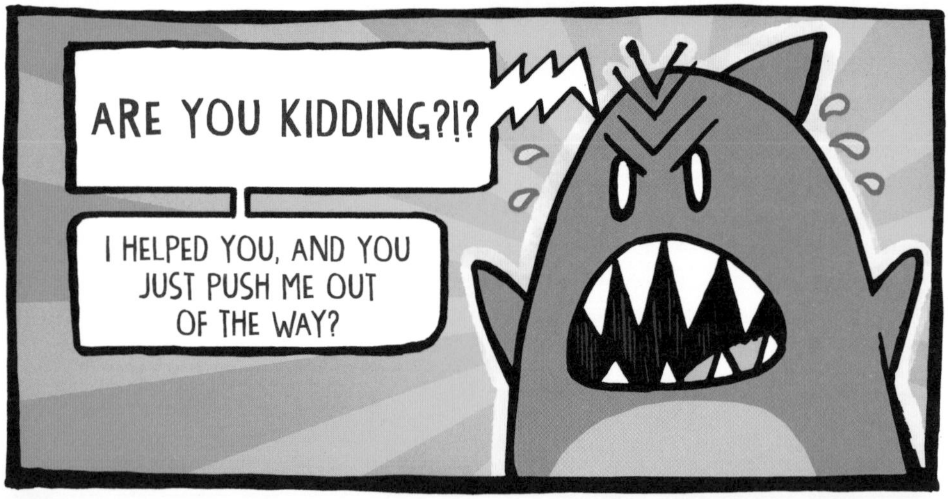
ARE YOU KIDDING?!?
I HELPED YOU, AND YOU JUST PUSH ME OUT OF THE WAY?

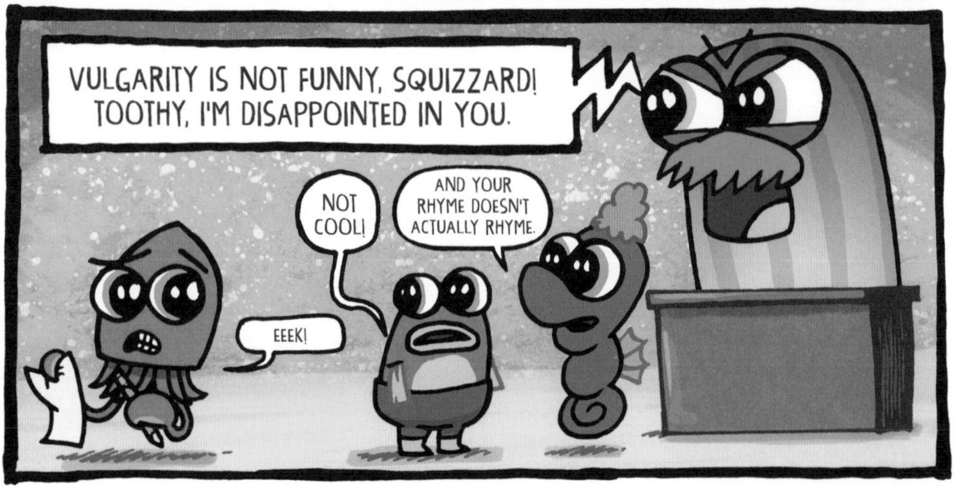
VULGARITY IS NOT FUNNY, SQUIZZARD! TOOTHY, I'M DISAPPOINTED IN YOU.
NOT COOL!
AND YOUR RHYME DOESN'T ACTUALLY RHYME.
EEEK!

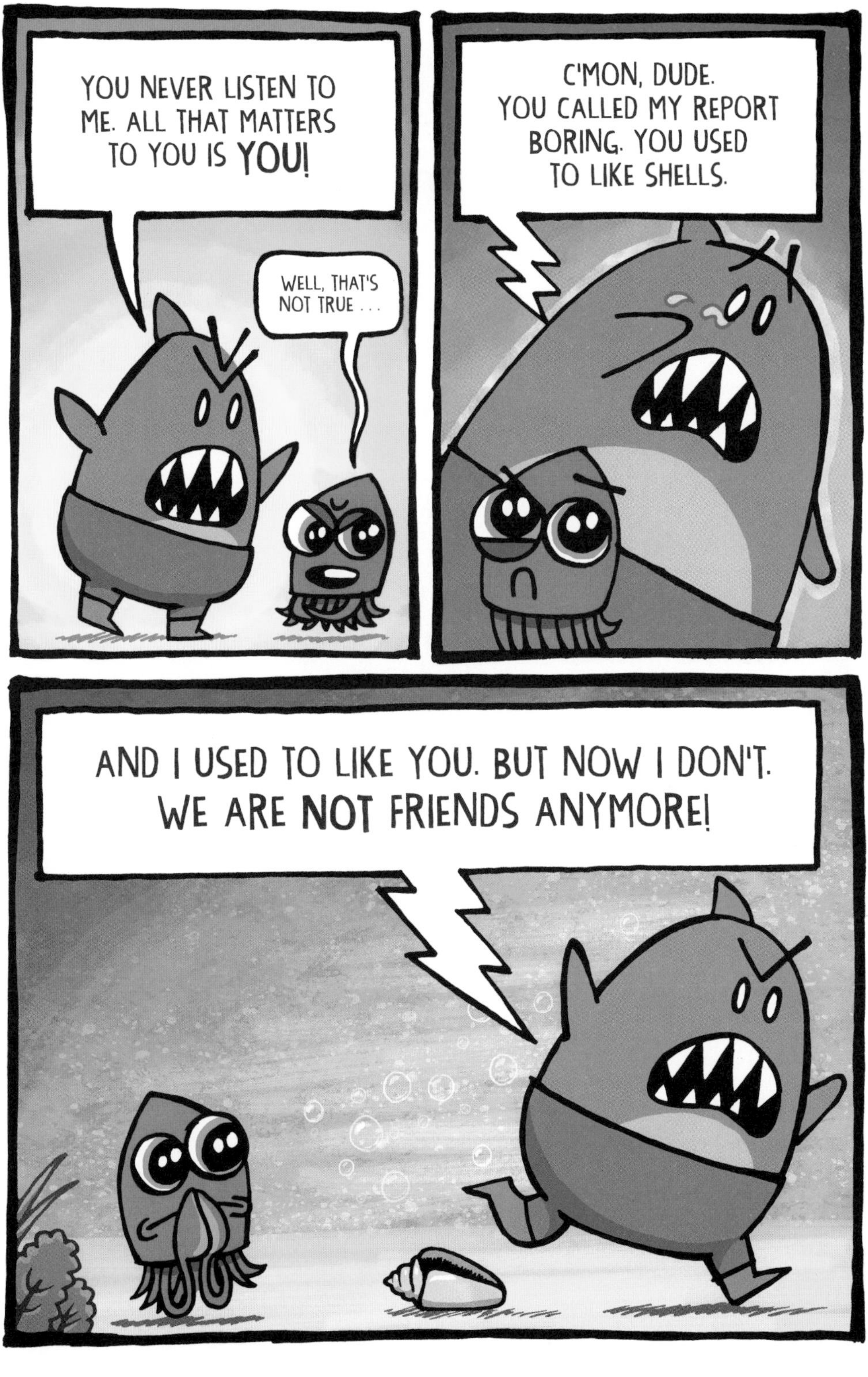
YOU NEVER LISTEN TO ME. ALL THAT MATTERS TO YOU IS YOU!
WELL, THAT'S NOT TRUE . . .
C'MON, DUDE. YOU CALLED MY REPORT BORING. YOU USED TO LIKE SHELLS.
AND I USED TO LIKE YOU. BUT NOW I DON'T. WE ARE NOT FRIENDS ANYMORE!

CHAPTER 3

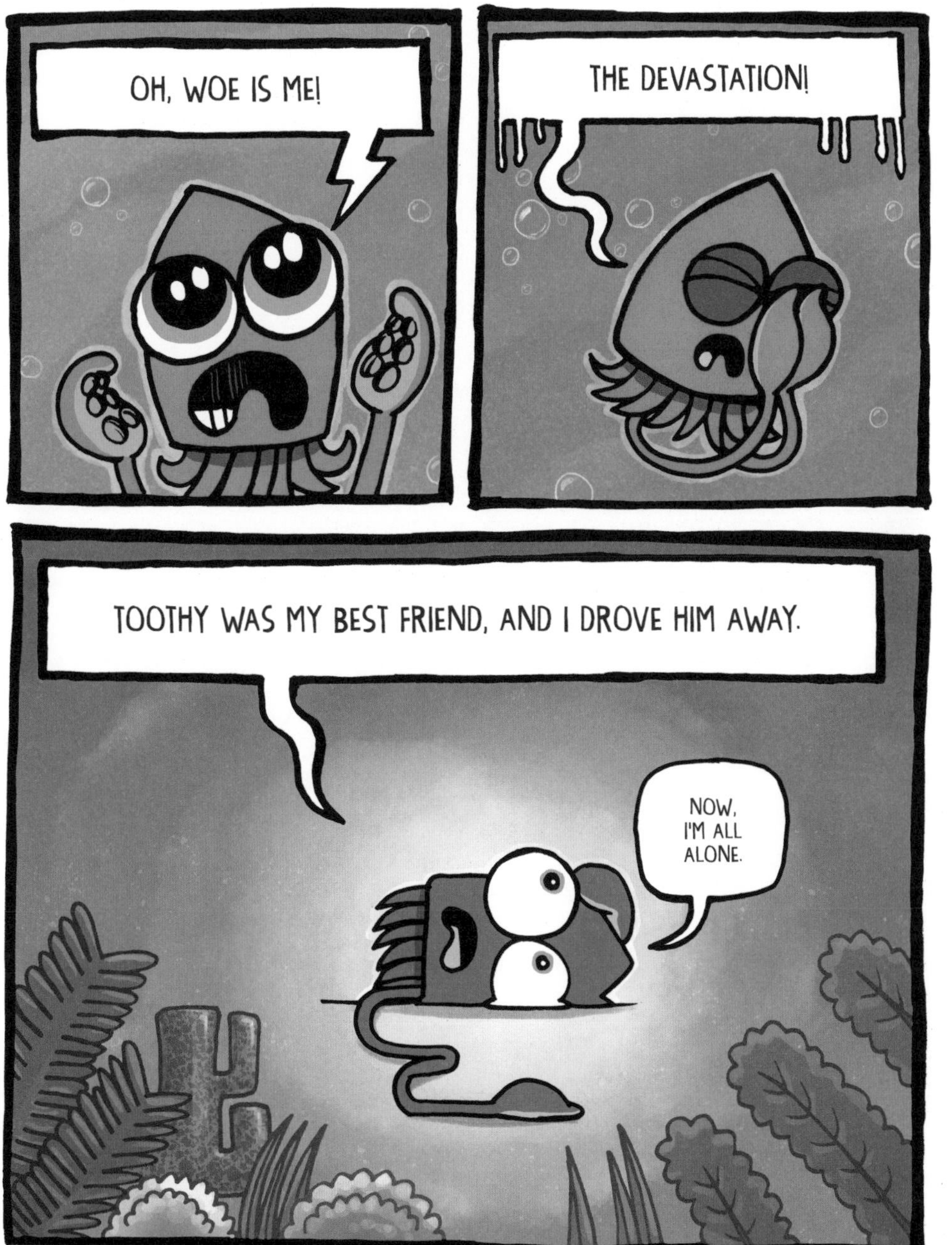
OH, WOE IS ME!
THE DEVASTATION!
TOOTHY WAS MY BEST FRIEND, AND I DROVE HIM AWAY.
NOW, I'M ALL ALONE.

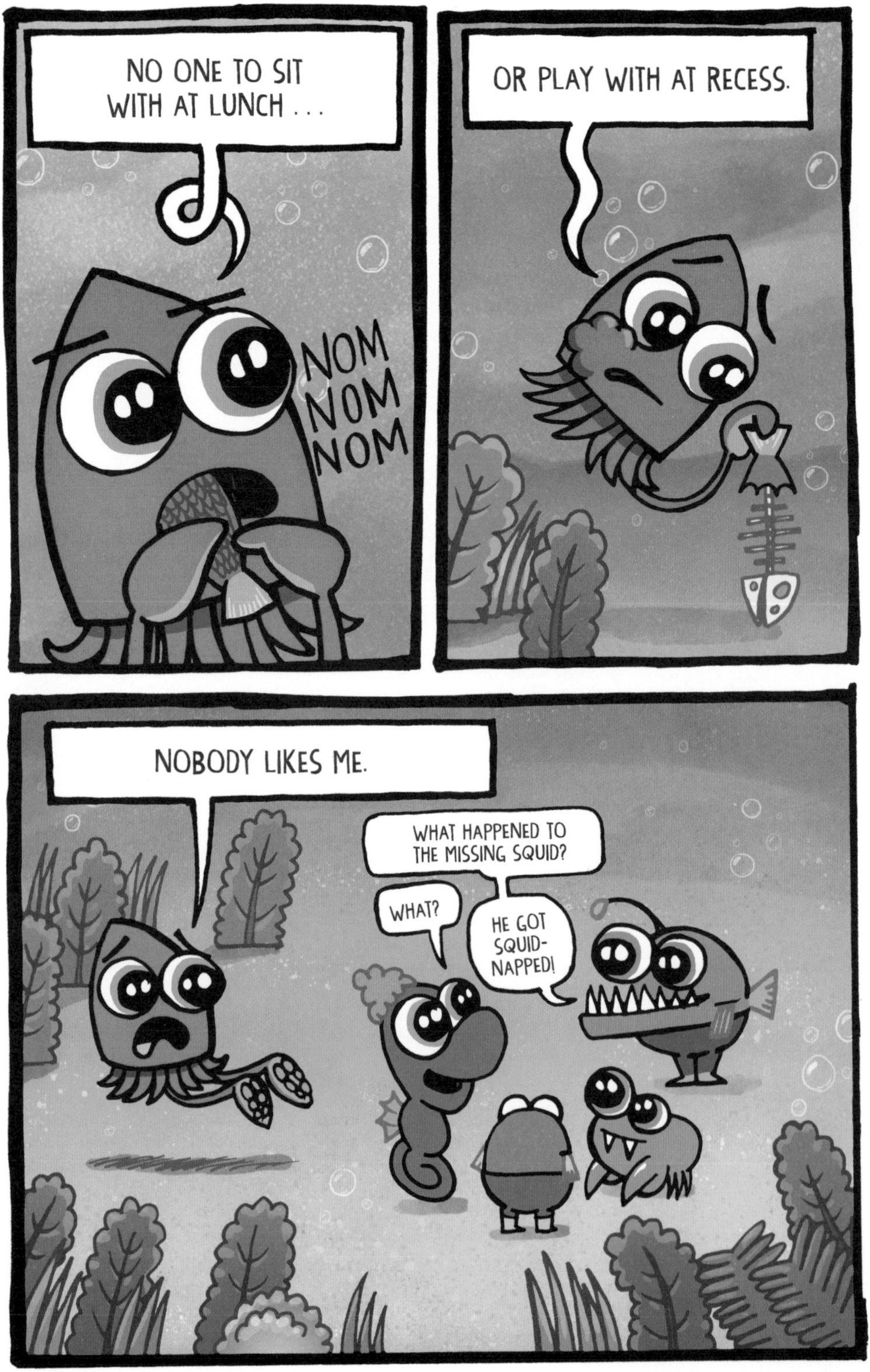
NO ONE TO SIT
WITH AT LUNCH . . .
NOM
NOM
NOM
OR PLAY WITH AT RECESS.
NOBODY LIKES ME.
WHAT HAPPENED TO
THE MISSING SQUID?
WHAT?
HE GOT
SQUID-
NAPPED!

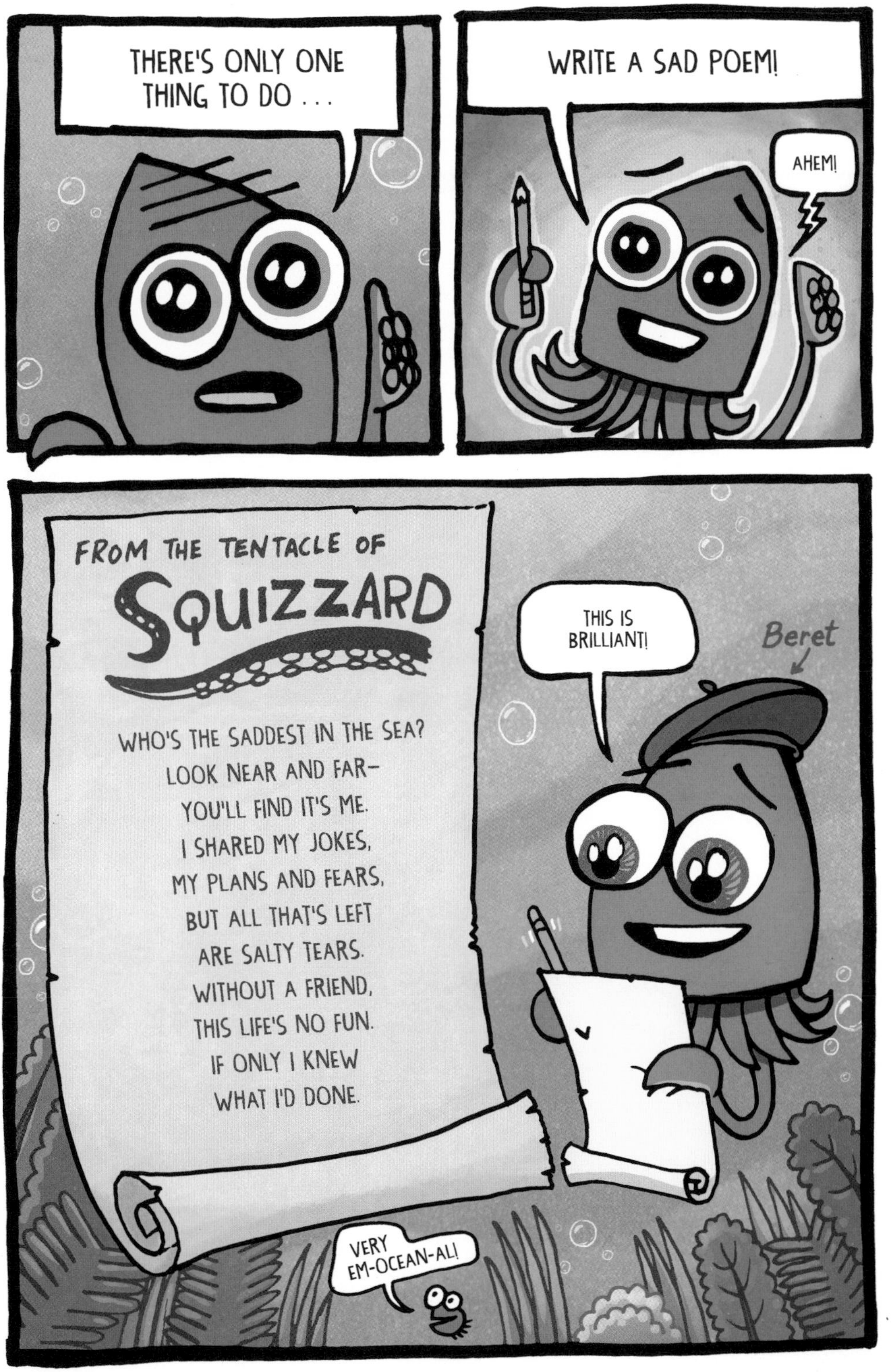
THERE'S ONLY ONE THING TO DO . . .
WRITE A SAD POEM!
AHEM!
FROM THE TENTACLE OF
SQUIZZARD
WHO'S THE SADDEST IN THE SEA?
LOOK NEAR AND FAR—
YOU'LL FIND IT'S ME.
I SHARED MY JOKES,
MY PLANS AND FEARS,
BUT ALL THAT'S LEFT
ARE SALTY TEARS.
WITHOUT A FRIEND,
THIS LIFE'S NO FUN.
IF ONLY I KNEW
WHAT I'D DONE.
THIS IS BRILLIANT!
Beret
VERY EM-OCEAN-AL!

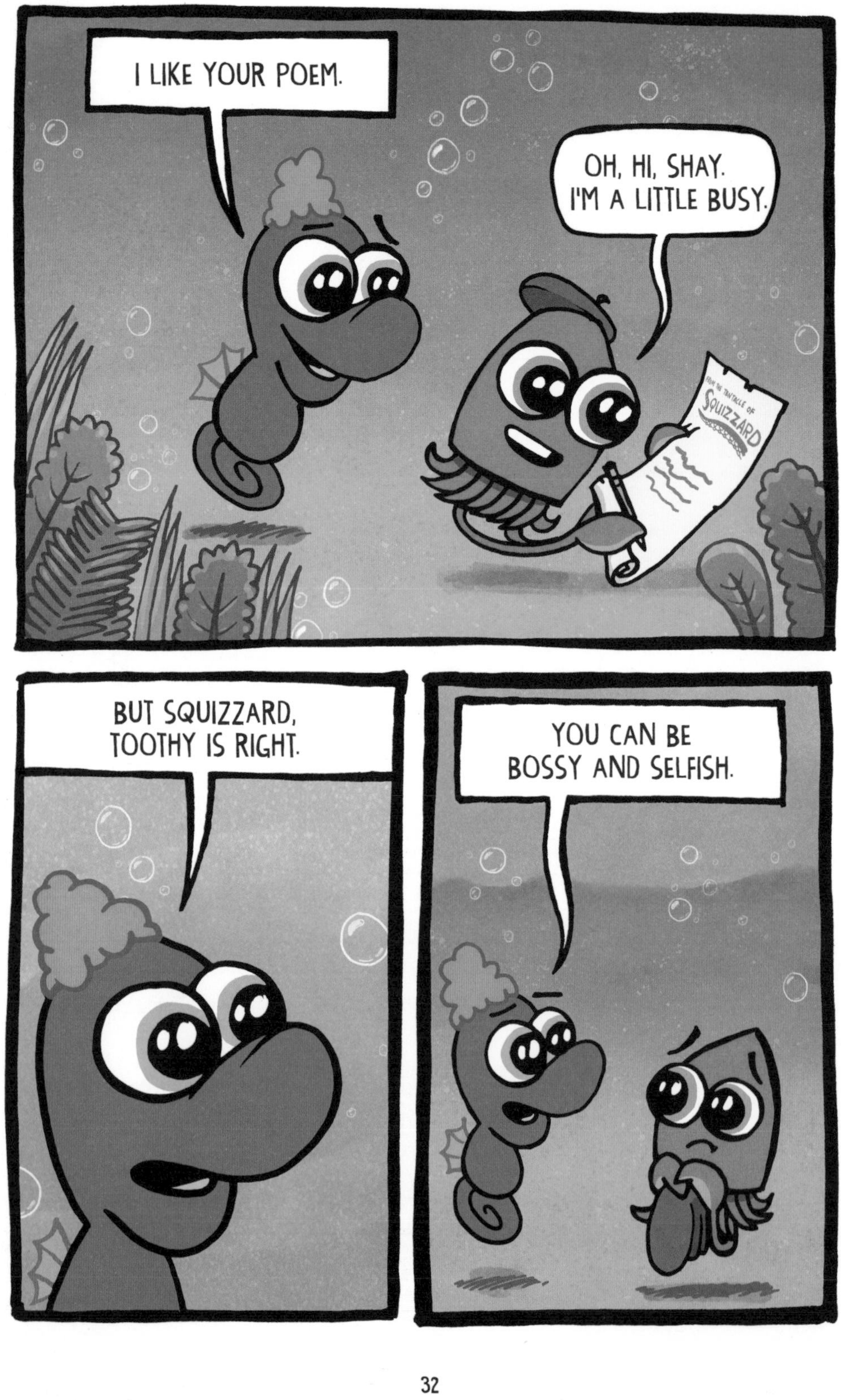
I LIKE YOUR POEM.
OH, HI, SHAY. I'M A LITTLE BUSY.
SQUIZZARD
BUT SQUIZZARD, TOOTHY IS RIGHT.
YOU CAN BE BOSSY AND SELFISH.

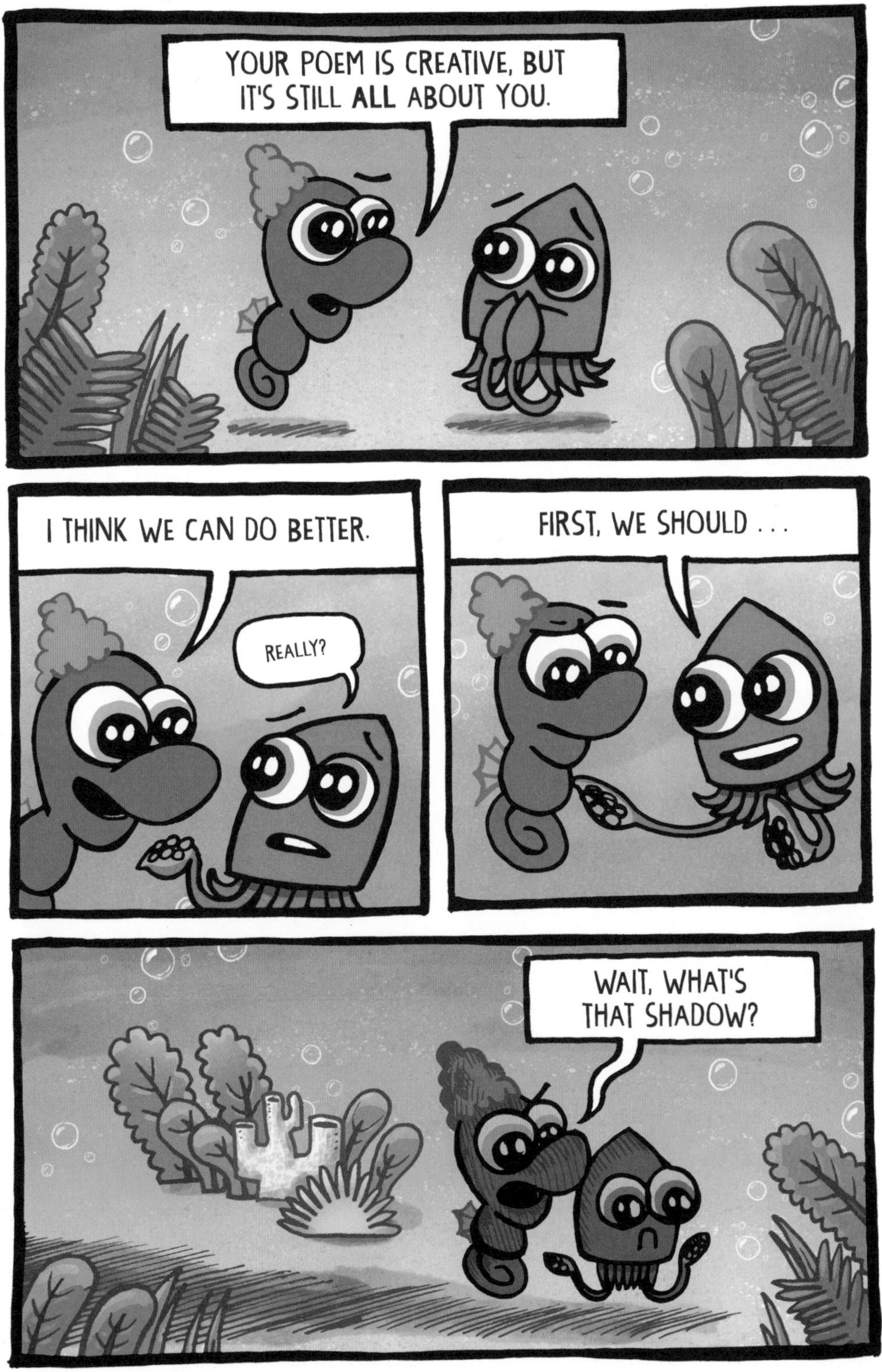
YOUR POEM IS CREATIVE, BUT IT'S STILL ALL ABOUT YOU.
I THINK WE CAN DO BETTER.
REALLY?
FIRST, WE SHOULD . . .
WAIT, WHAT'S THAT SHADOW?

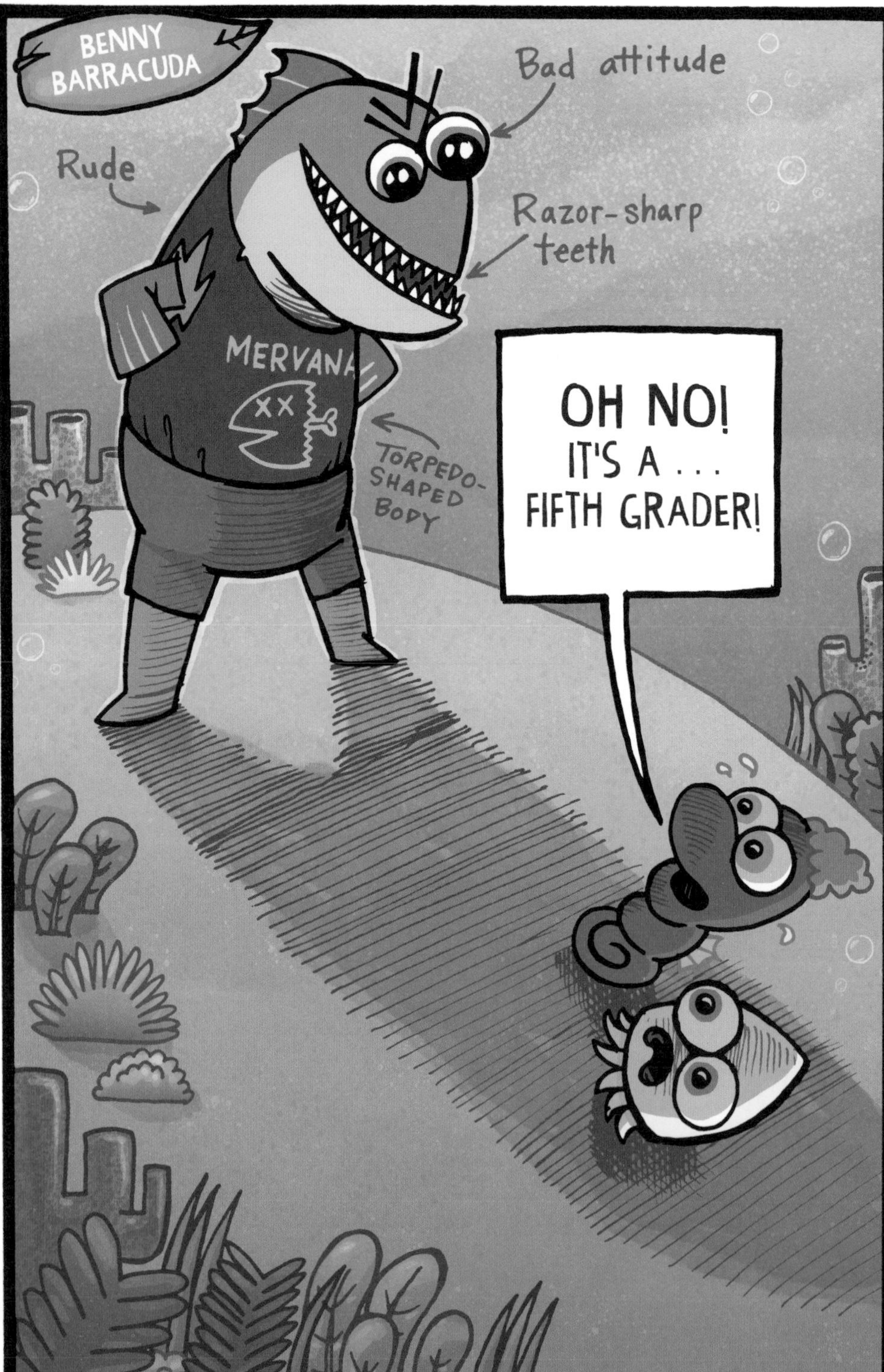
BENNY BARRACUDA
Bad attitude
Rude
Razor-sharp teeth
MERVANA
TORPEDO-SHAPED BODY
OH NO! IT'S A . . . FIFTH GRADER!

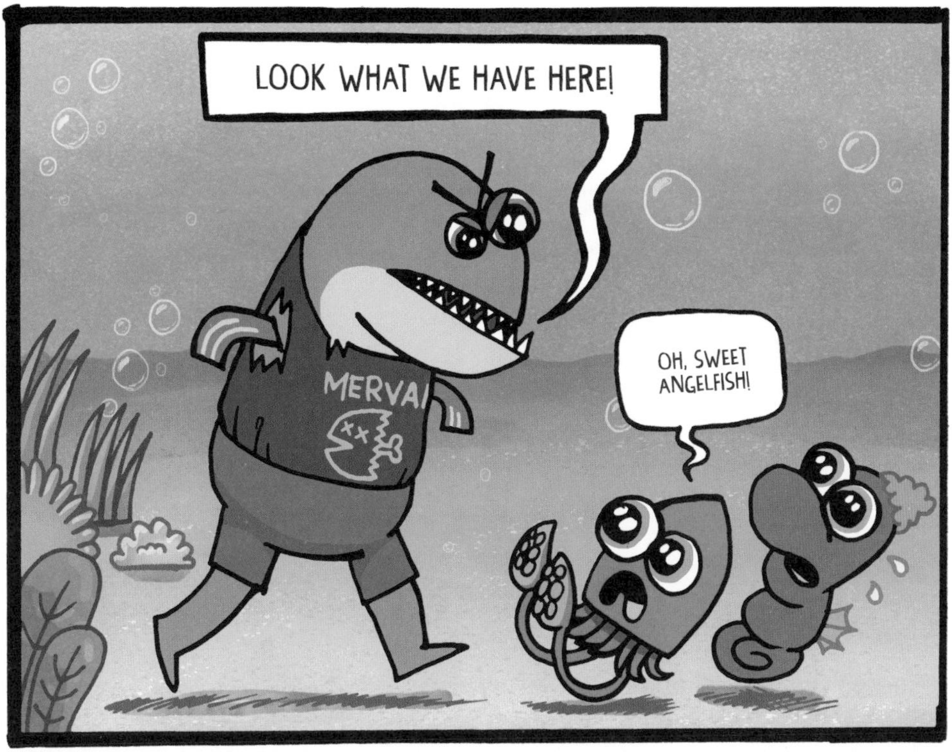
LOOK WHAT WE HAVE HERE!
OH, SWEET ANGELFISH!
MERVA

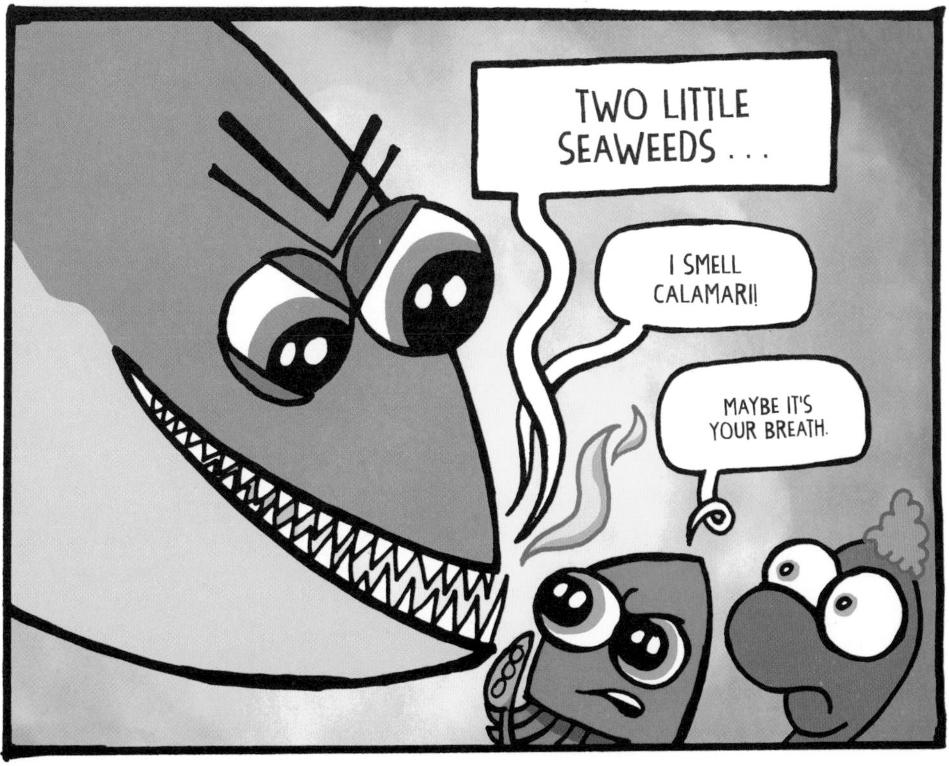
TWO LITTLE SEAWEEDS . . .
I SMELL CALAMARI!
MAYBE IT'S YOUR BREATH.

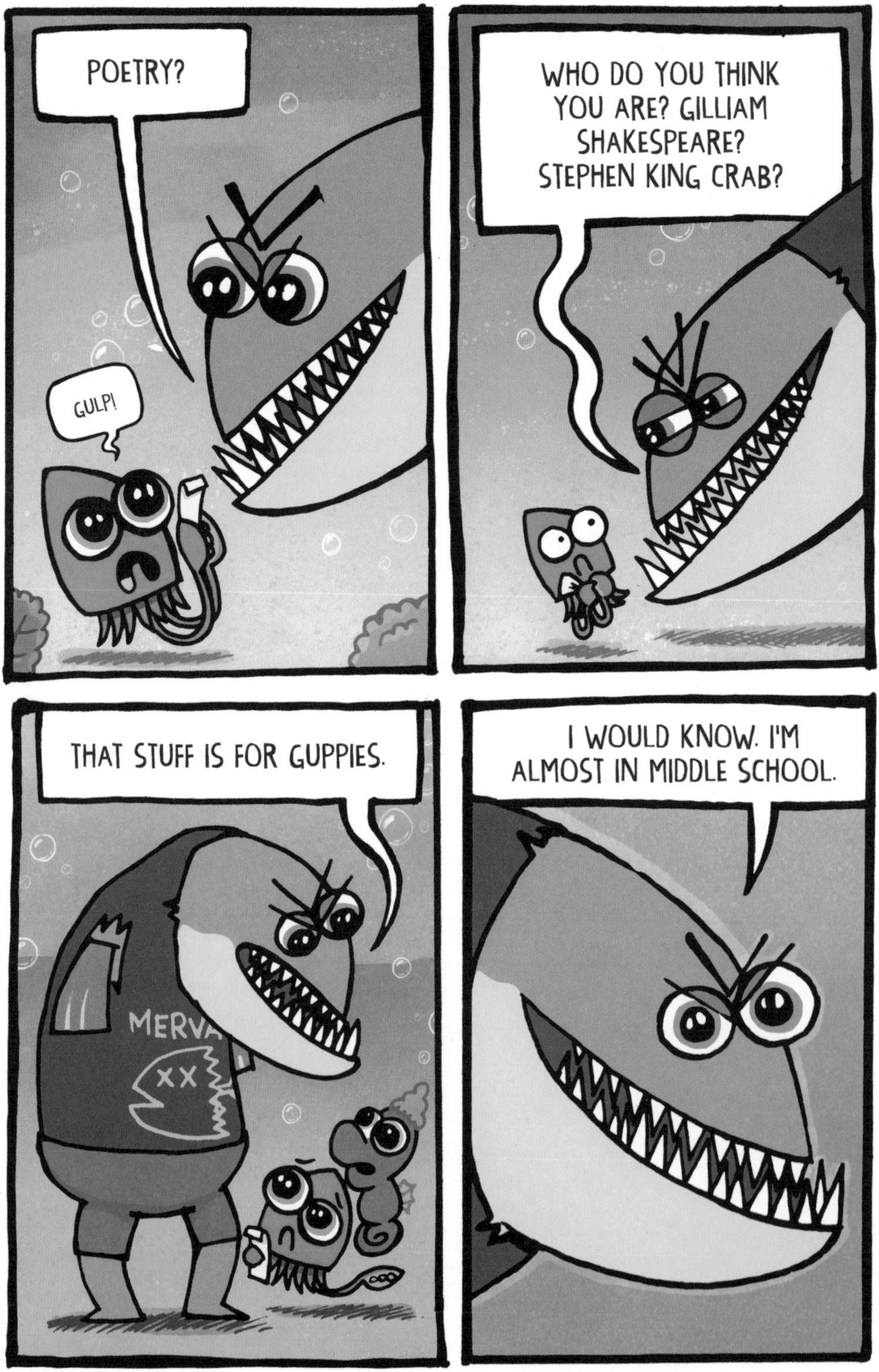

POETRY?
GULP!
WHO DO YOU THINK YOU ARE? GILLIAM SHAKESPEARE? STEPHEN KING CRAB?
THAT STUFF IS FOR GUPPIES.
MERVA
XX
I WOULD KNOW. I'M ALMOST IN MIDDLE SCHOOL.

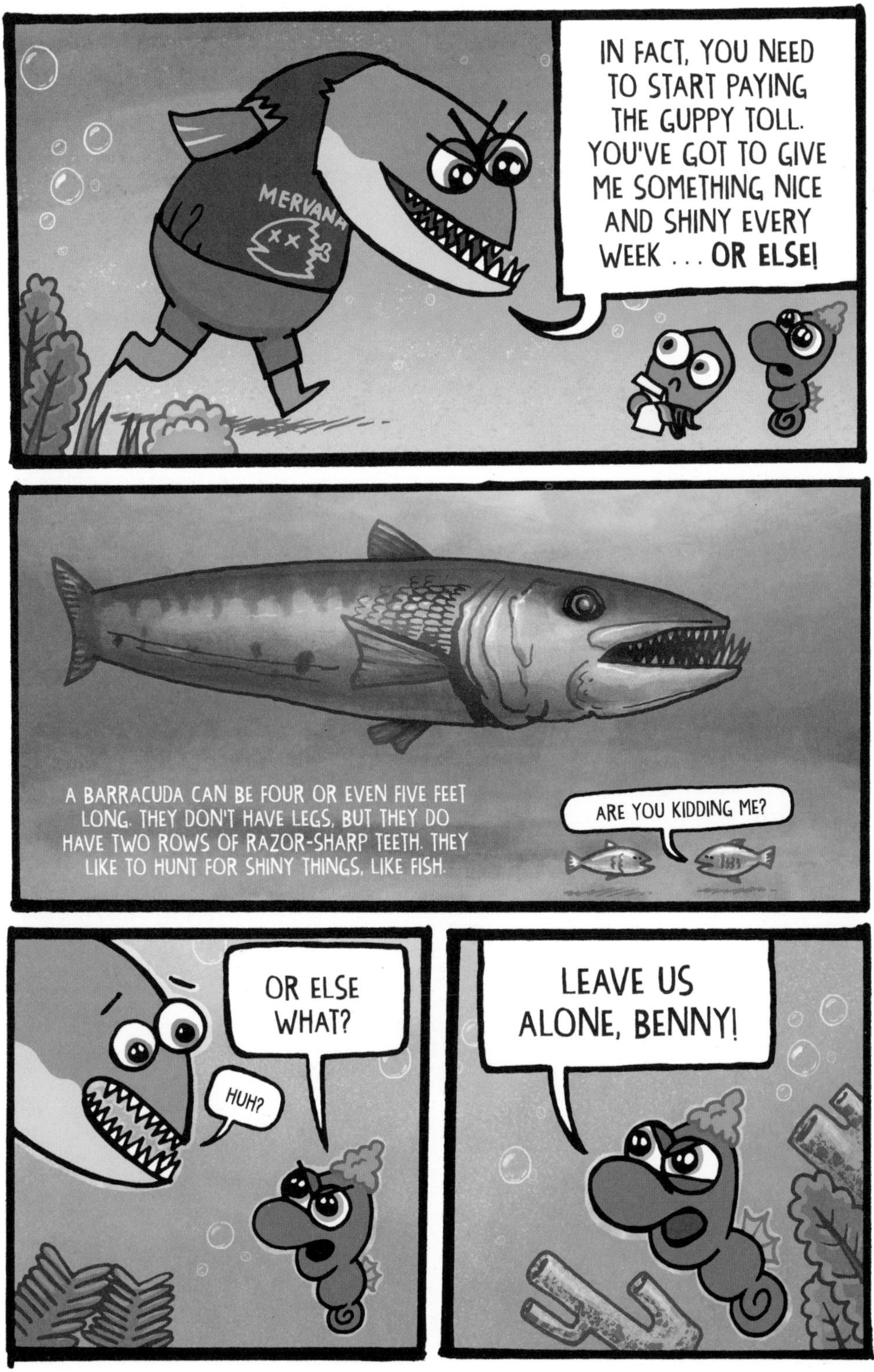
IN FACT, YOU NEED TO START PAYING THE GUPPY TOLL. YOU'VE GOT TO GIVE ME SOMETHING NICE AND SHINY EVERY WEEK . . . **OR ELSE!**
MERVANA
A BARRACUDA CAN BE FOUR OR EVEN FIVE FEET LONG. THEY DON'T HAVE LEGS, BUT THEY DO HAVE TWO ROWS OF RAZOR-SHARP TEETH. THEY LIKE TO HUNT FOR SHINY THINGS, LIKE FISH.
ARE YOU KIDDING ME?
OR ELSE WHAT?
HUH?
LEAVE US ALONE, BENNY!

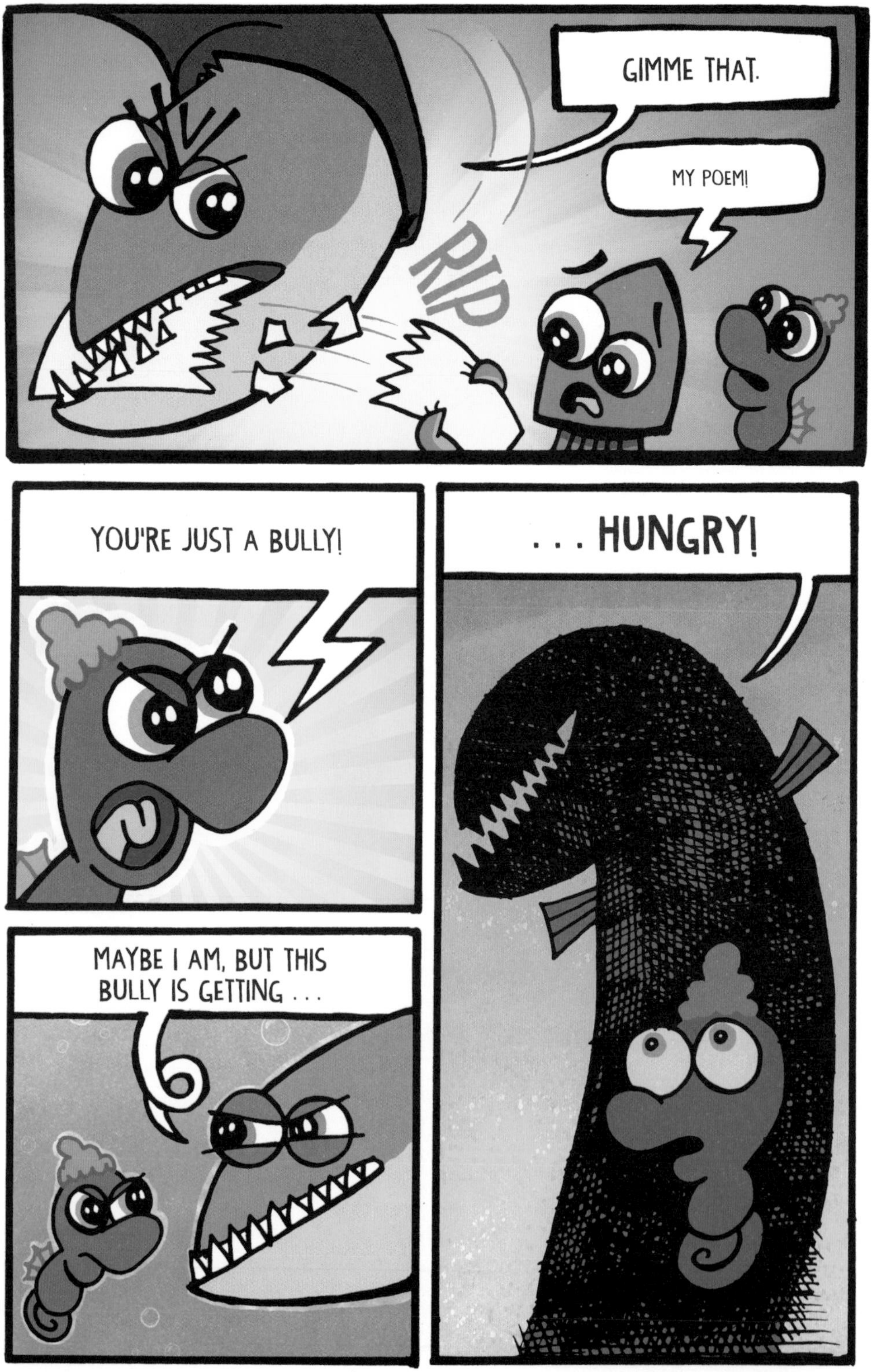
GIMME THAT.
MY POEM!
RIP
YOU'RE JUST A BULLY!
MAYBE I AM, BUT THIS BULLY IS GETTING . . .
. . . HUNGRY!

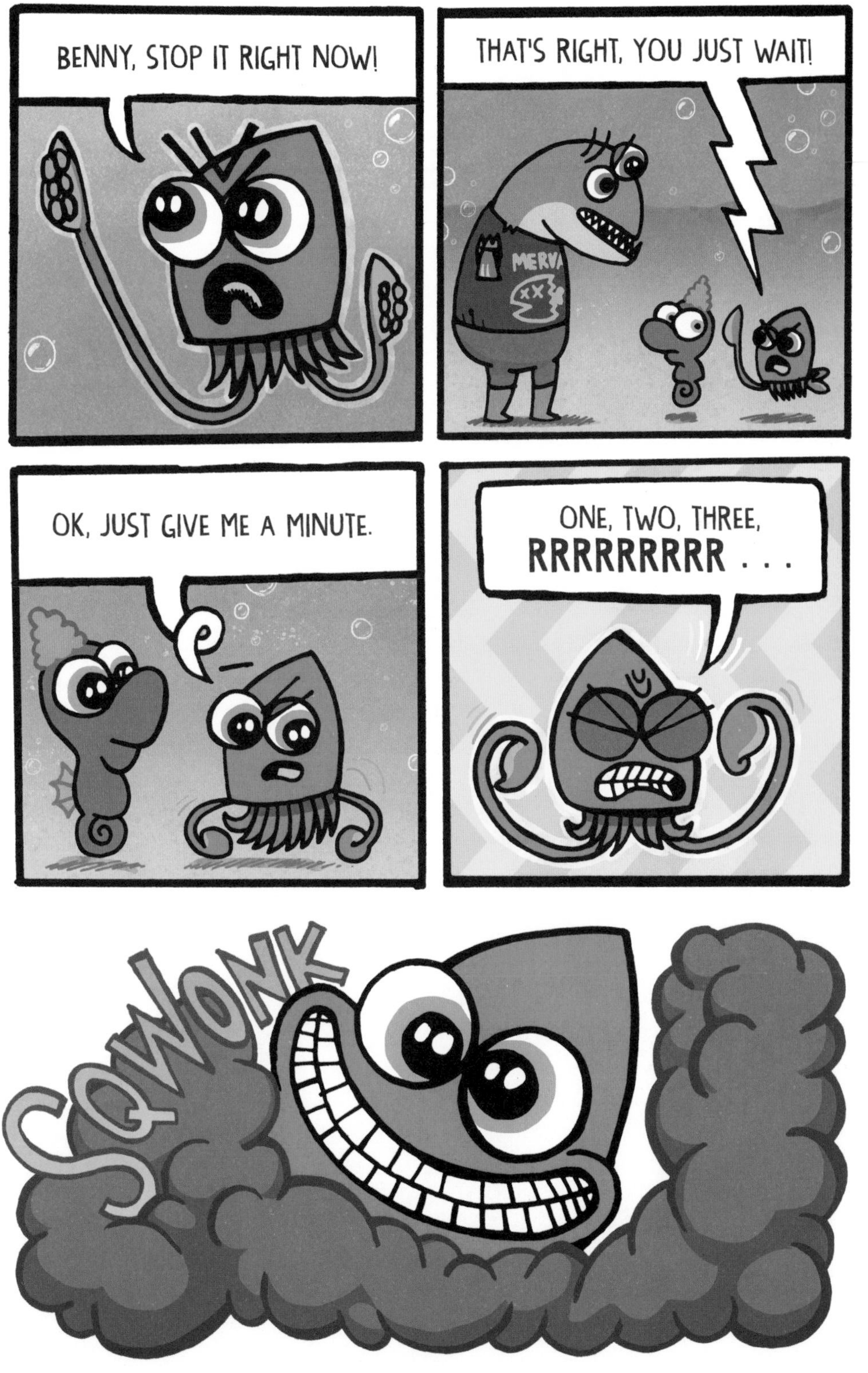
BENNY, STOP IT RIGHT NOW!
THAT'S RIGHT, YOU JUST WAIT!
MERV
OK, JUST GIVE ME A MINUTE.
ONE, TWO, THREE,
RRRRRRRRR . . .
SQWONK

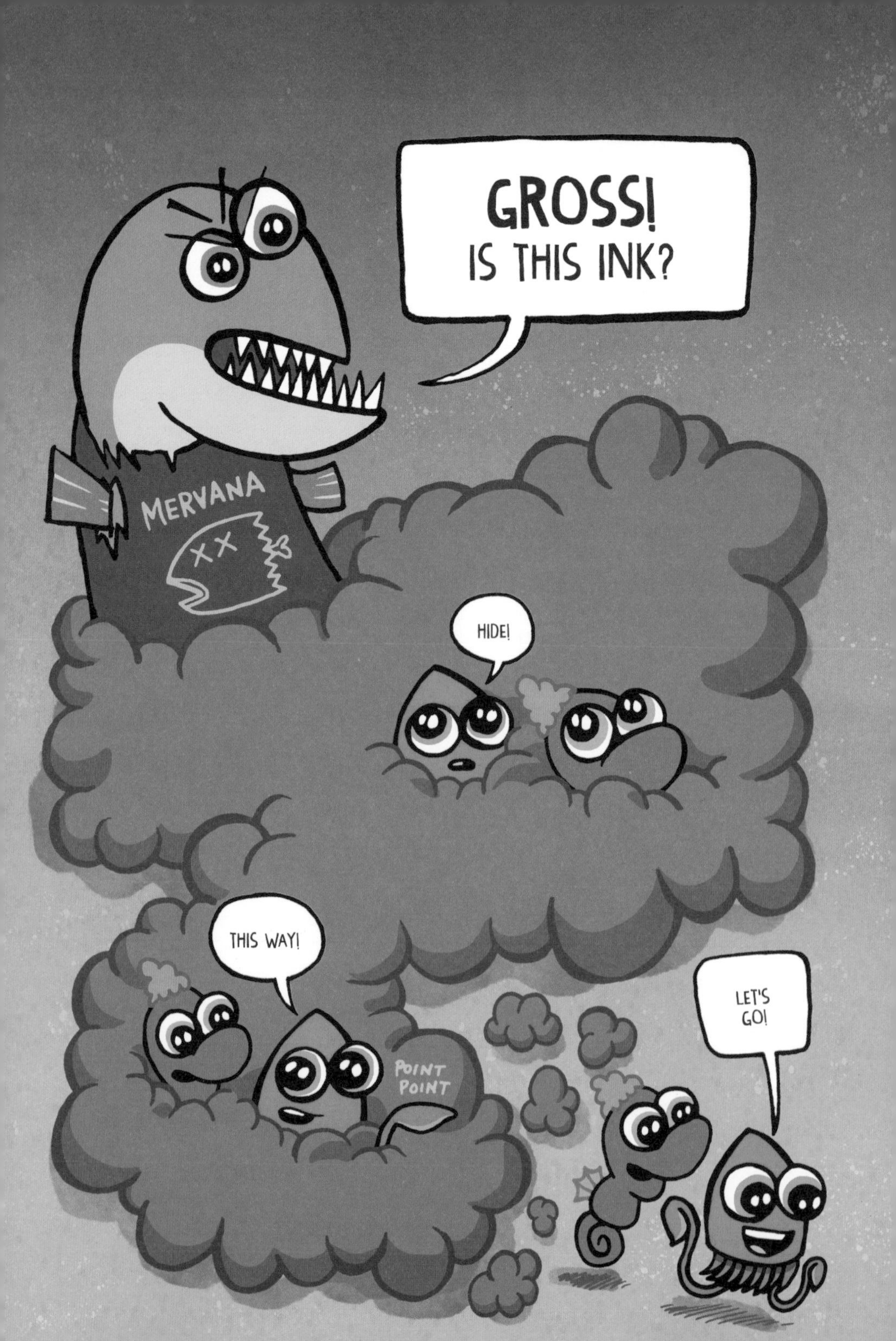
GROSS!
IS THIS INK?
MERVANA
HIDE!
THIS WAY!
POINT POINT
LET'S GO!

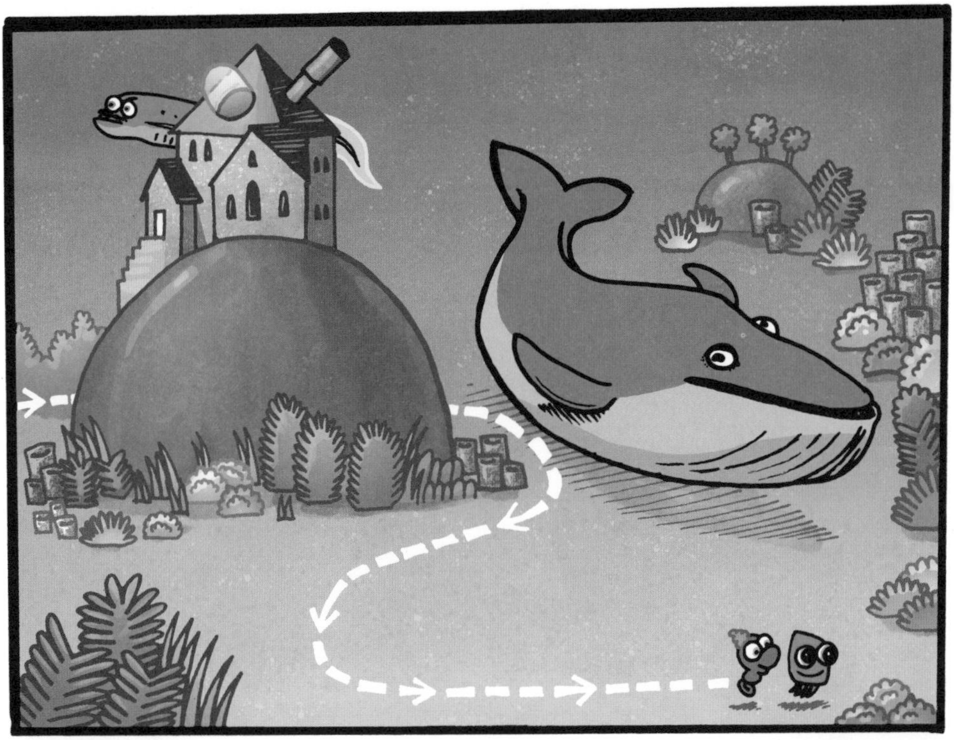

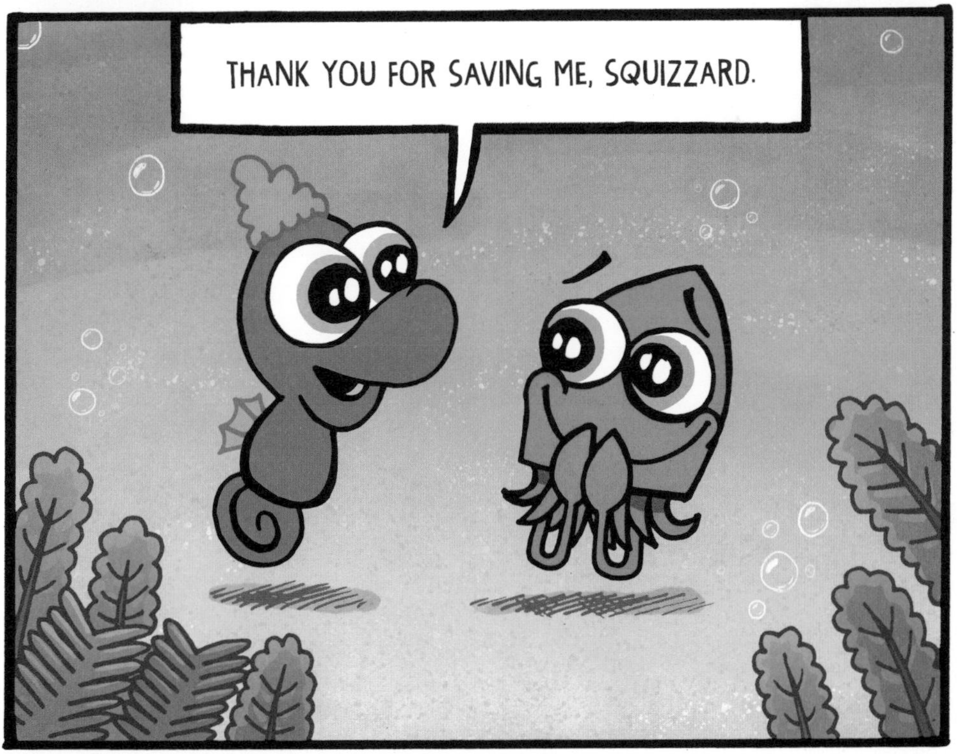
THANK YOU FOR SAVING ME, SQUIZZARD.

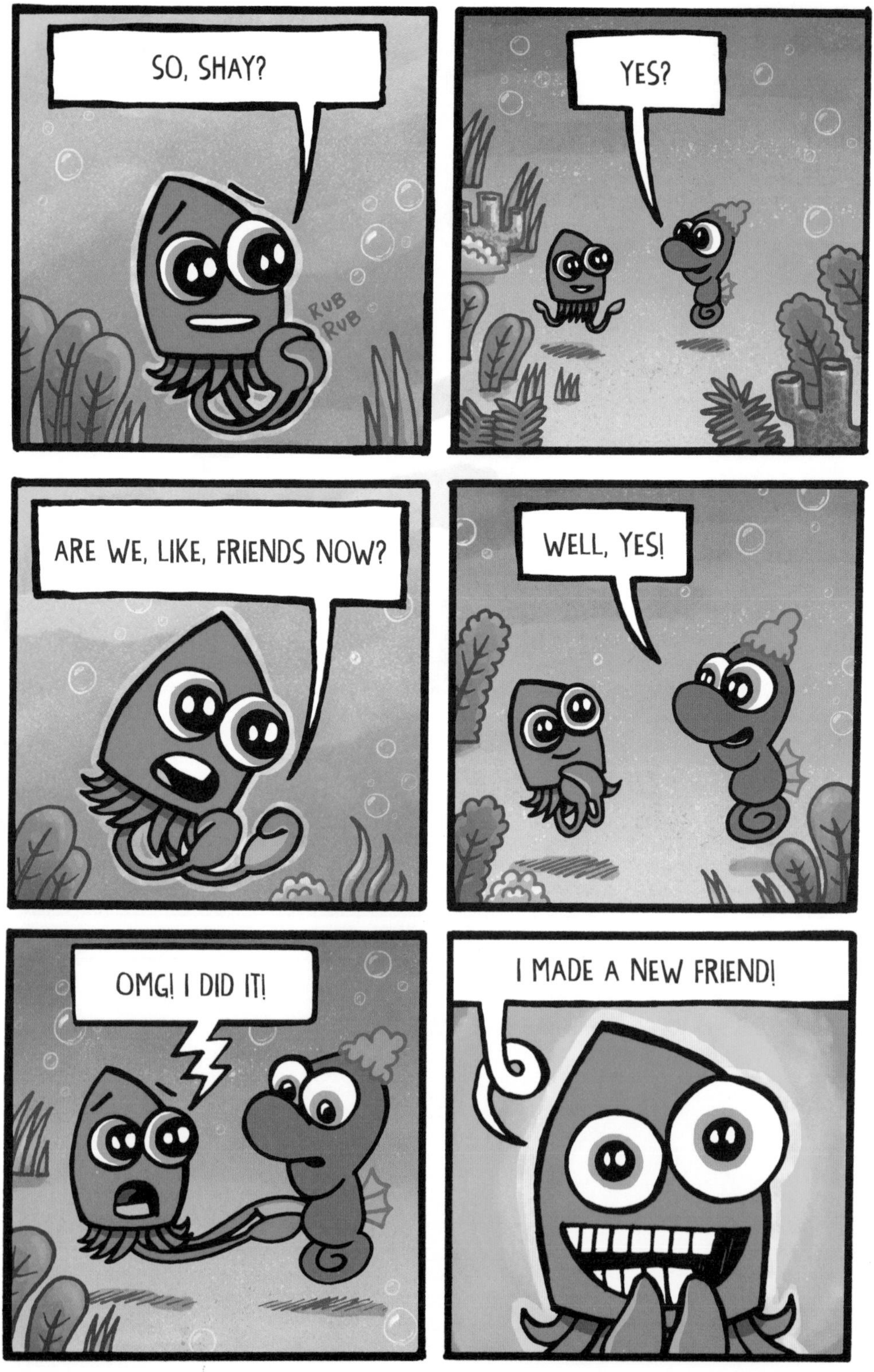
SO, SHAY?
RUB RUB
YES?
ARE WE, LIKE, FRIENDS NOW?
WELL, YES!
OMG! I DID IT!
I MADE A NEW FRIEND!

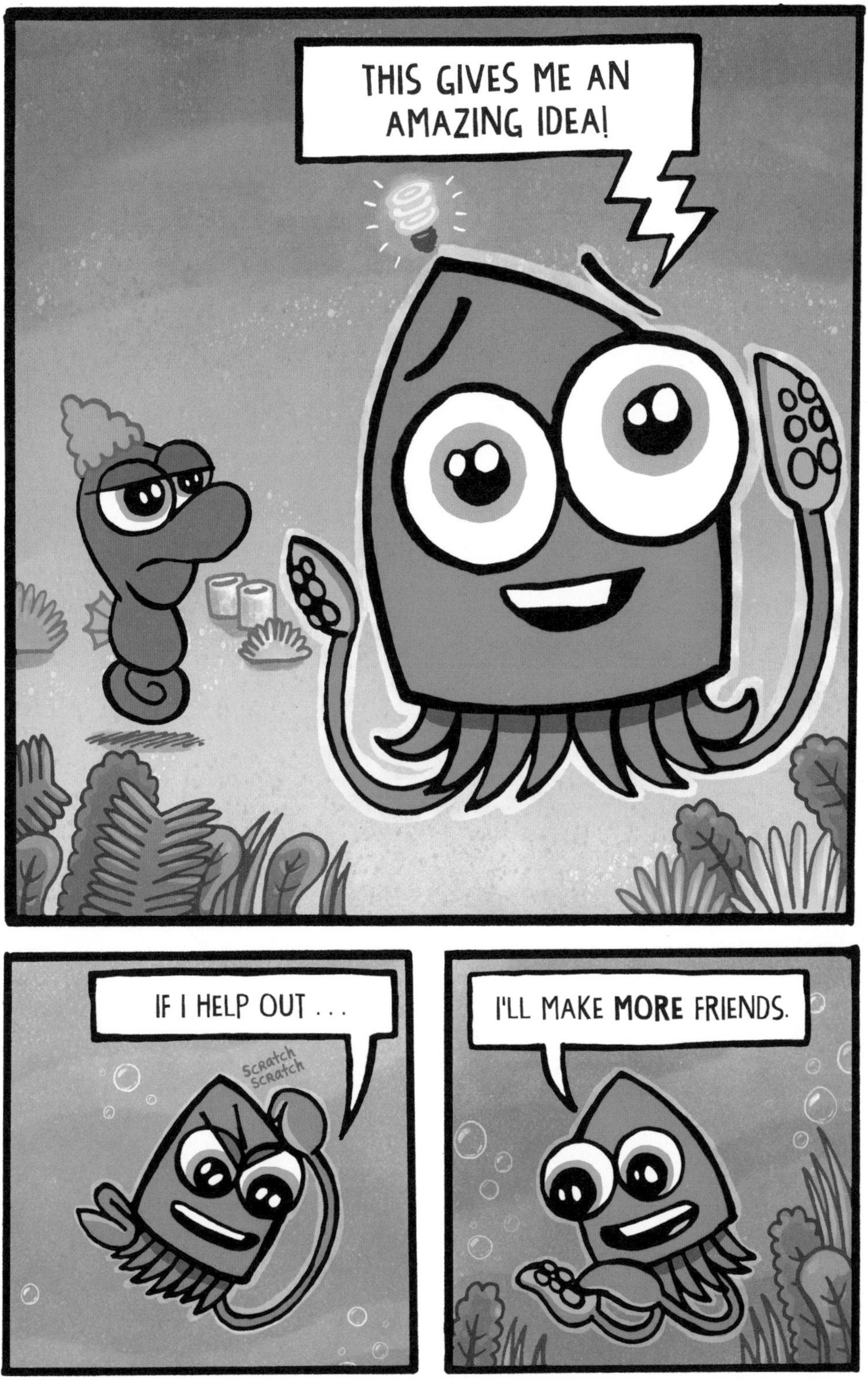
THIS GIVES ME AN AMAZING IDEA!
IF I HELP OUT . . .
SCRATCH SCRATCH
I'LL MAKE **MORE** FRIENDS.

CHAPTER 4

49

50

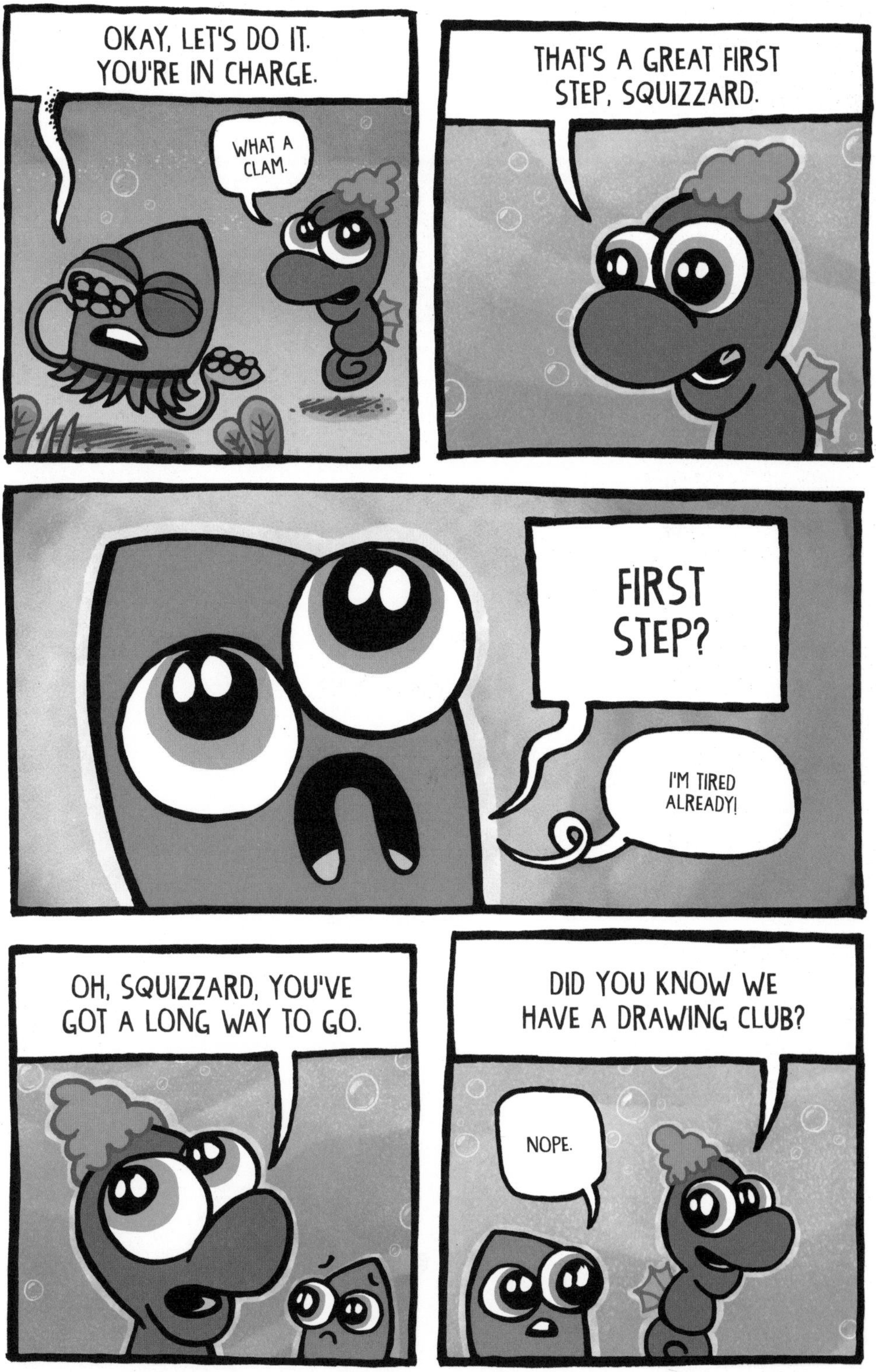
OKAY, LET'S DO IT. YOU'RE IN CHARGE.
WHAT A CLAM.
THAT'S A GREAT FIRST STEP, SQUIZZARD.
FIRST STEP?
I'M TIRED ALREADY!
OH, SQUIZZARD, YOU'VE GOT A LONG WAY TO GO.
DID YOU KNOW WE HAVE A DRAWING CLUB?
NOPE.

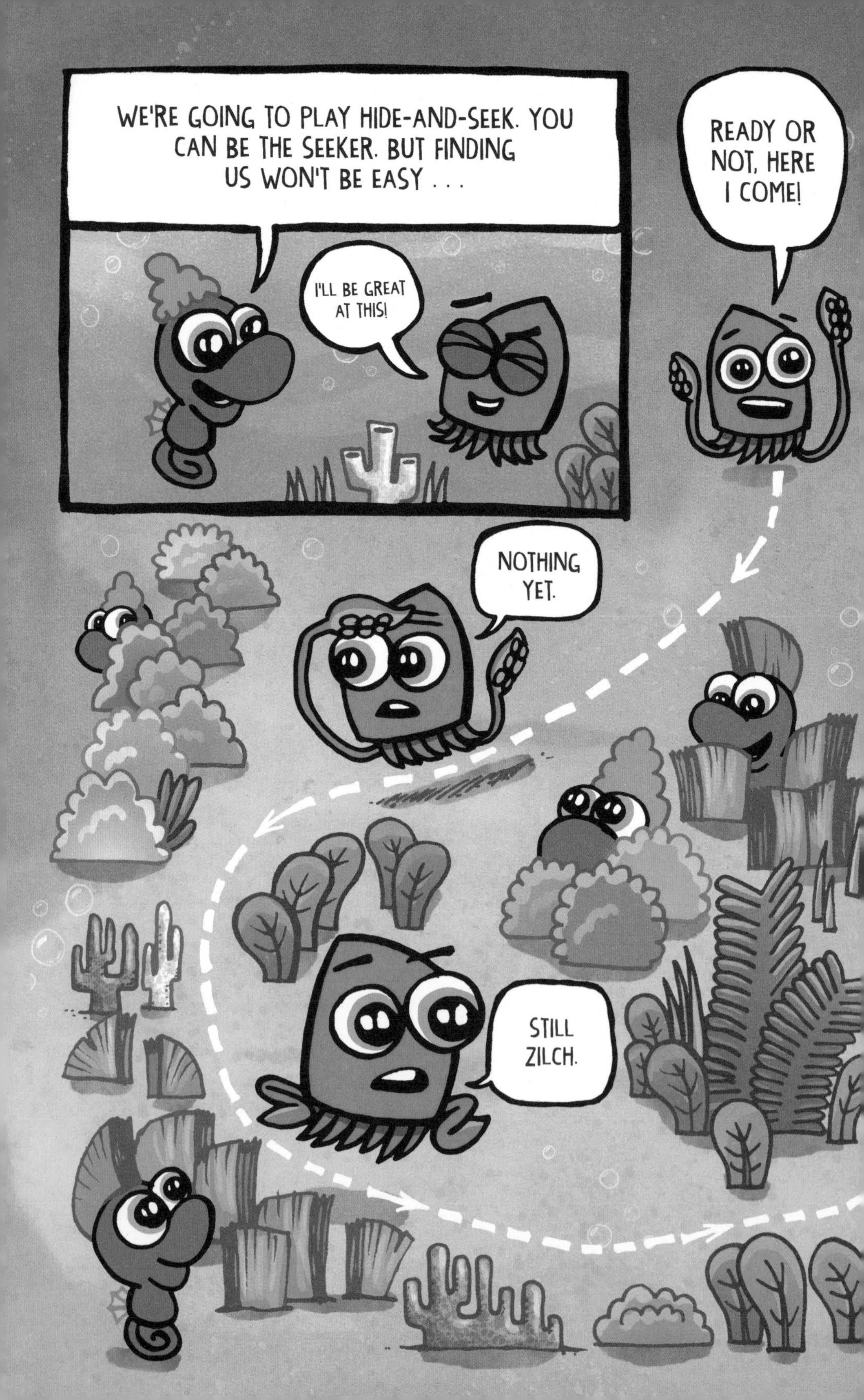
WE'RE GOING TO PLAY HIDE-AND-SEEK. YOU CAN BE THE SEEKER. BUT FINDING US WON'T BE EASY . . .
I'LL BE GREAT AT THIS!
READY OR NOT, HERE I COME!
NOTHING YET.
STILL ZILCH.

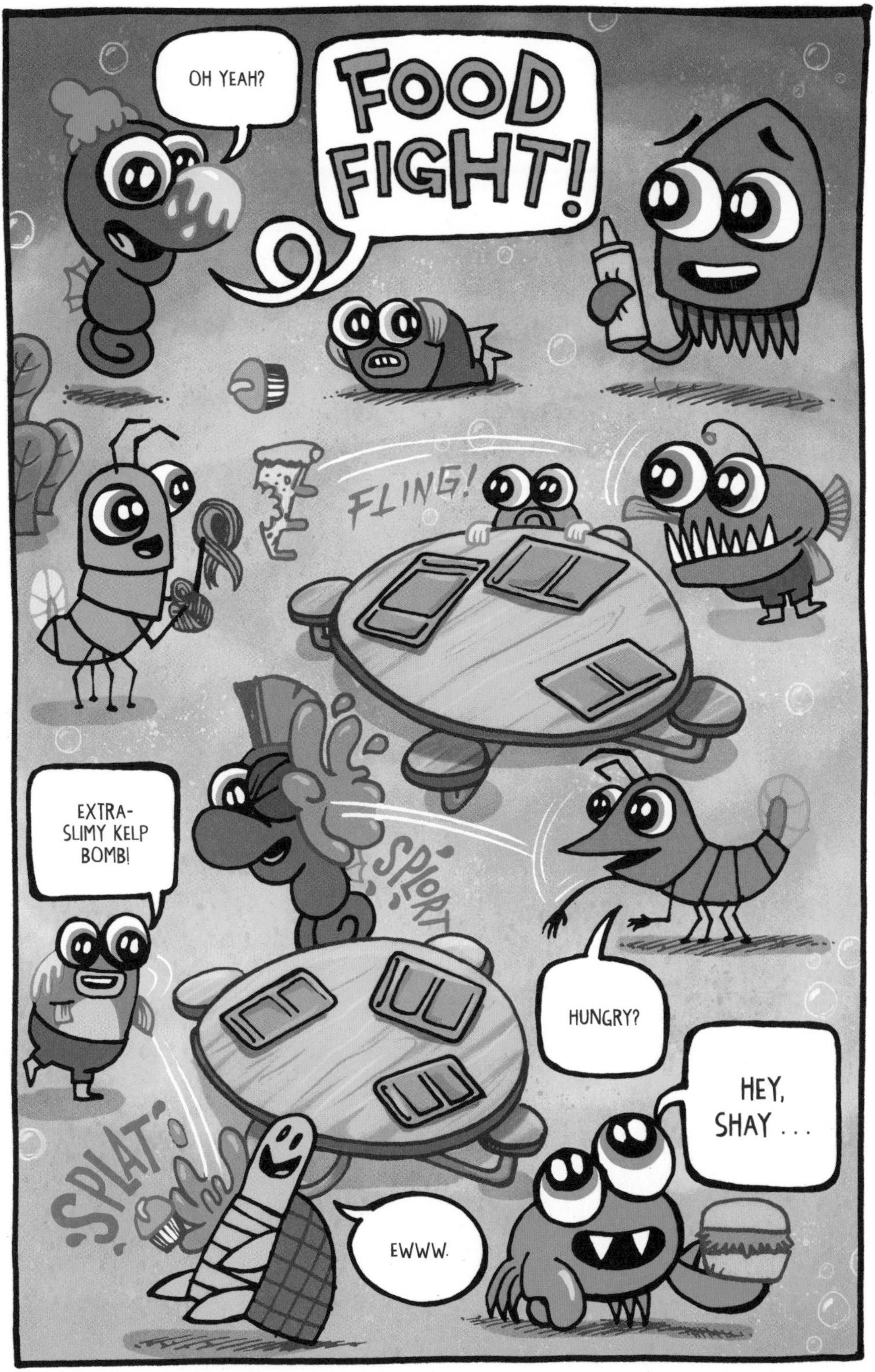
OH YEAH?
FOOD FIGHT!
FLING!
EXTRA-SLIMY KELP BOMB!
SPLORT
HUNGRY?
HEY, SHAY . . .
SPLAT
EWWW.

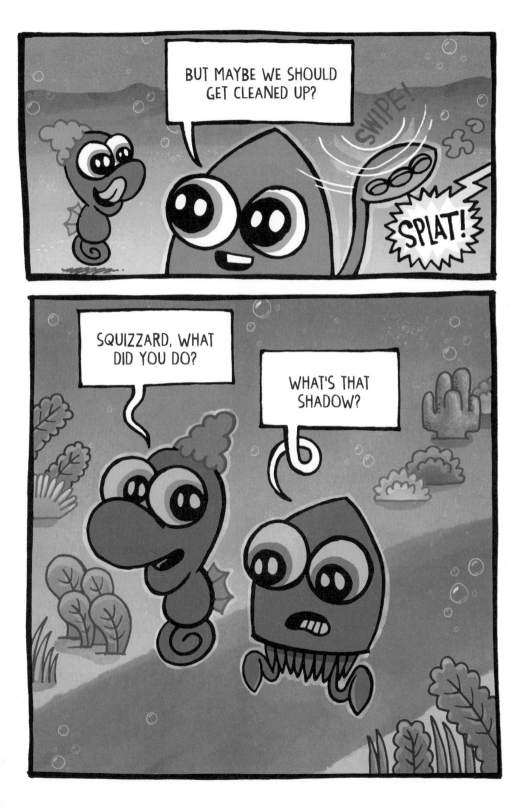

CHAPTER 5

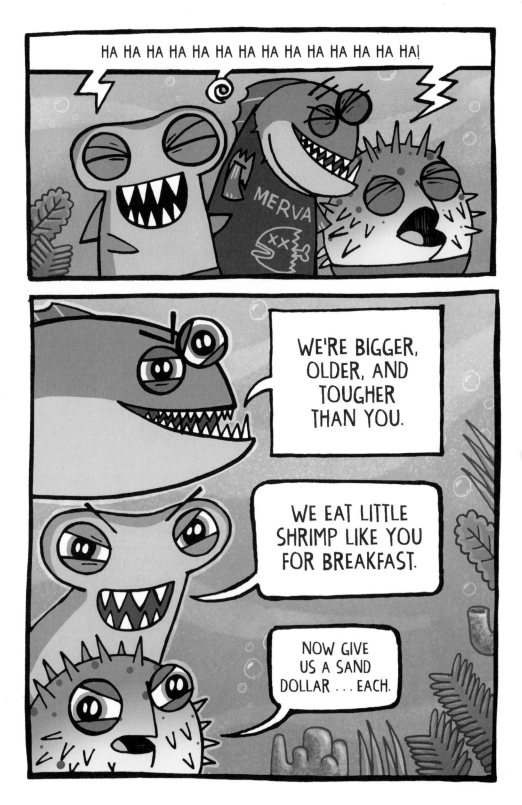

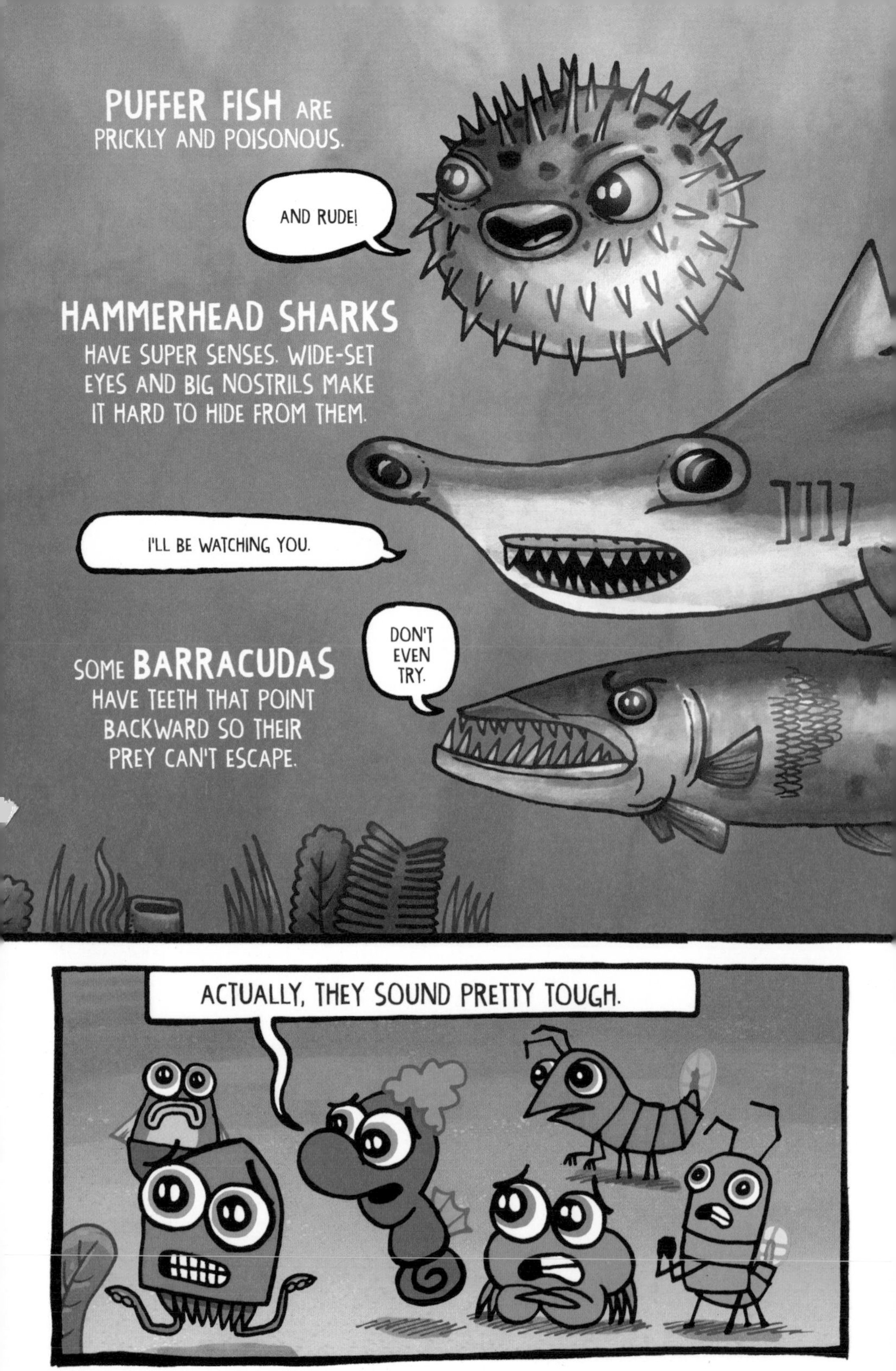
PUFFER FISH ARE PRICKLY AND POISONOUS.
AND RUDE!
HAMMERHEAD SHARKS HAVE SUPER SENSES. WIDE-SET EYES AND BIG NOSTRILS MAKE IT HARD TO HIDE FROM THEM.
I'LL BE WATCHING YOU.
SOME BARRACUDAS HAVE TEETH THAT POINT BACKWARD SO THEIR PREY CAN'T ESCAPE.
DON'T EVEN TRY.
ACTUALLY, THEY SOUND PRETTY TOUGH.

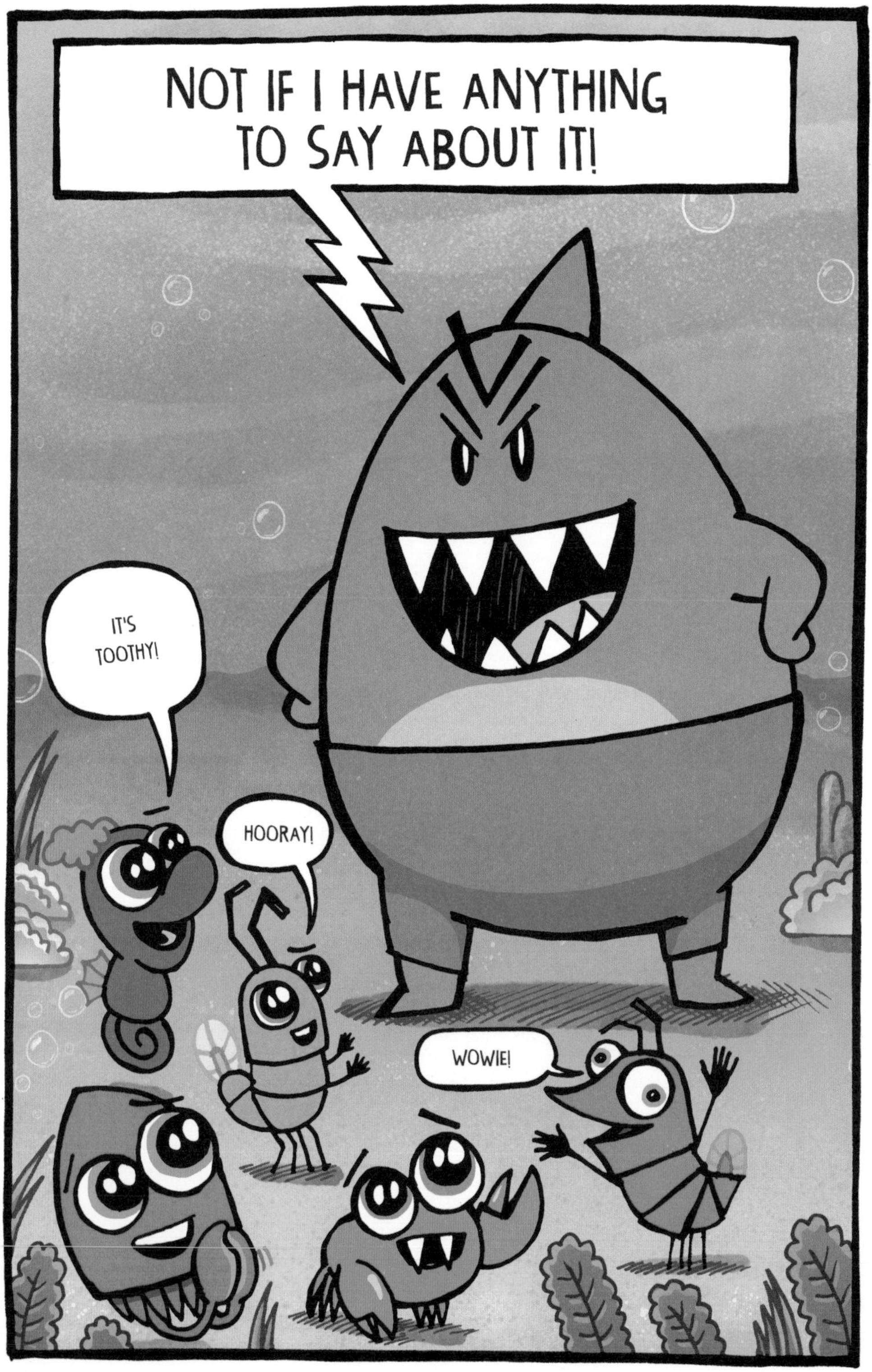
NOT IF I HAVE ANYTHING TO SAY ABOUT IT!
IT'S TOOTHY!
HOORAY!
WOWIE!

78

CHAPTER 6

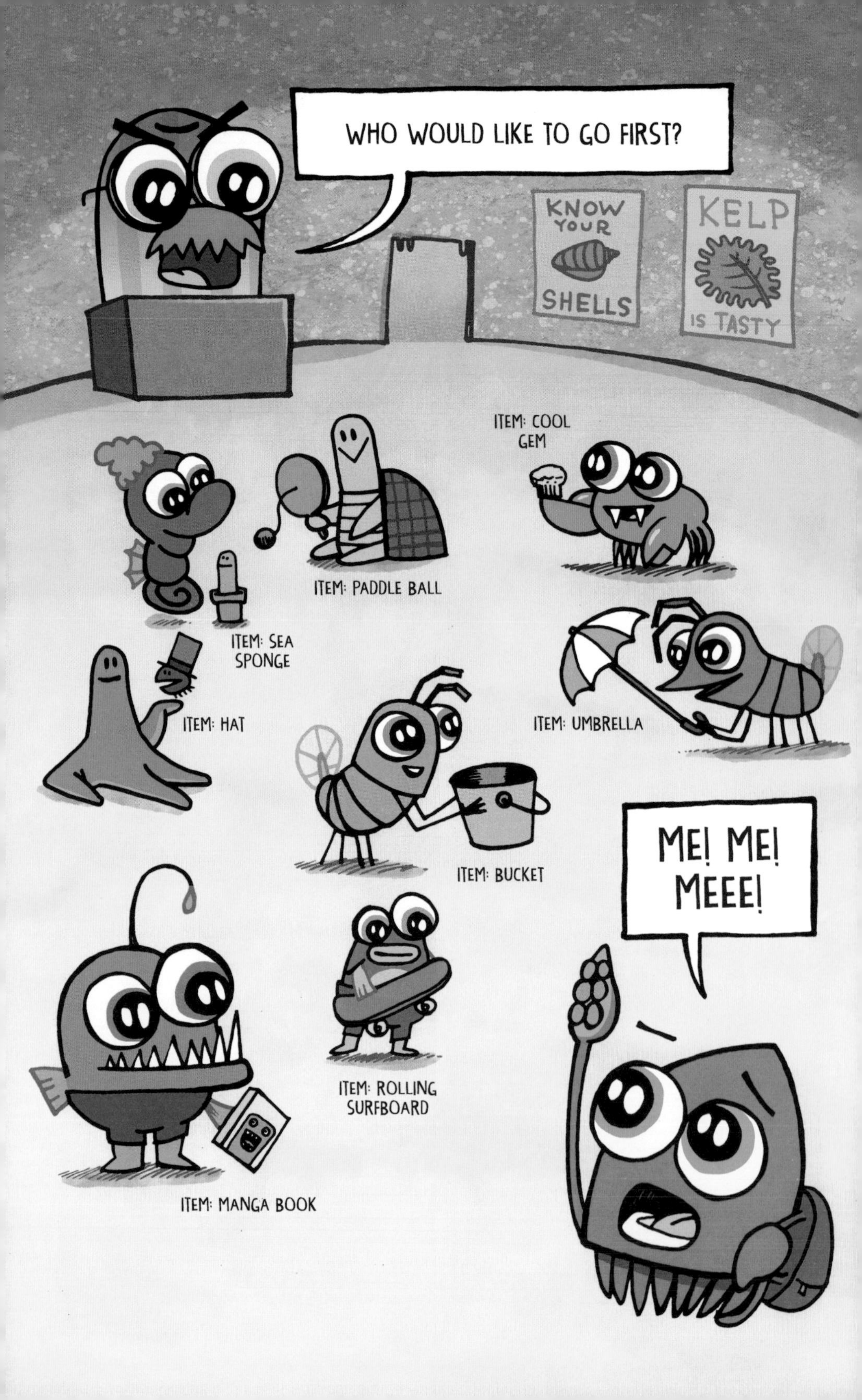
WHO WOULD LIKE TO GO FIRST?
KNOW YOUR SHELLS
KELP IS TASTY
ITEM: COOL GEM
ITEM: PADDLE BALL
ITEM: SEA SPONGE
ITEM: HAT
ITEM: UMBRELLA
ITEM: BUCKET
ME! ME! MEEE!
ITEM: ROLLING SURFBOARD
ITEM: MANGA BOOK

83

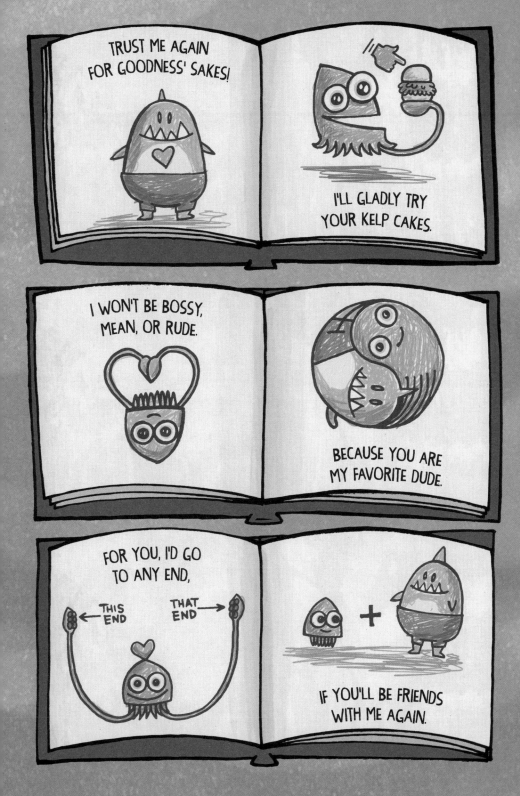

86

FRIENDSHIP UNDER THE SEA

There are around one million different kinds of animals living in the ocean. Some of those animals hunt each other, but others live together in peace.

When two creatures live closely together for a long period of time, they share a bond that's called symbiosis (sim-be-OH-sis). Sometimes this bond can be helpful for both creatures.

For example, clown fish like to hide inside a sea anemone because the anemone protects it from predators. In return, the clown fish cleans the anemone and gets rid of harmful parasites.

And when a blind pistol shrimp burrows down into the mud to forage for food, a little goby comes along to act as a bodyguard, but also to find a safe place to store its eggs.

We can't know how animals really feel, but I'm pretty sure anyone would call Squizzard and Toothy's friendship totally symbiotic!

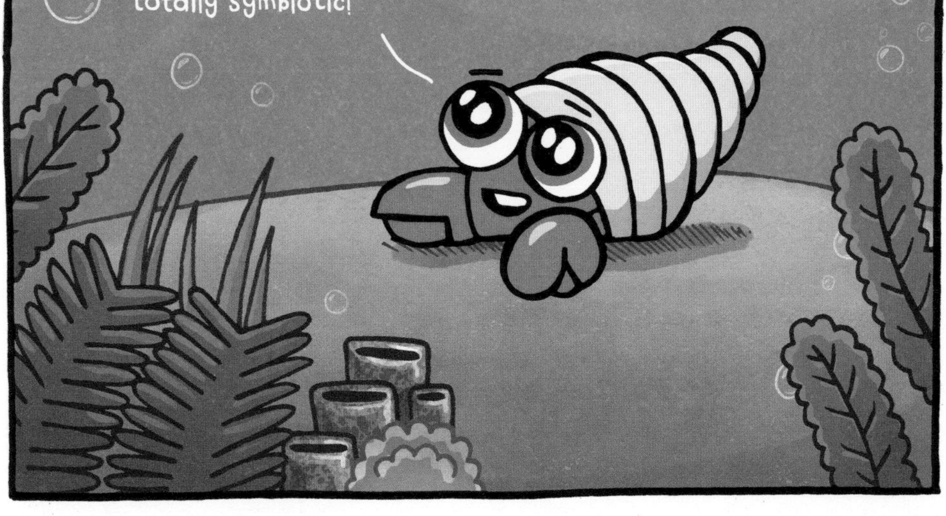

KEVIN SHERRY is the author and illustrator of many children's picture books, most notably The Yeti Files and Remy Sneakers series, and the picture book I'M THE BIGGEST THING IN THE OCEAN, which received starred reviews and won an original artwork award from the Society of Illustrators. He's a man of many interests: a chef, an avid cyclist and screen printer, and a performer of hilarious puppet shows for kids and adults. Kevin lives in Baltimore, Maryland.

ACKNOWLEDGMENTS

With thanks to Mom, Dad, Brian, Margie, Erin, Dale, Rachel, Ryan, Dan, Justin, Mary, Hunky Mr. Dev, Ed, Akiko Day, Jaclyn Wander Paris, and the Black Cherry Puppet Theater.

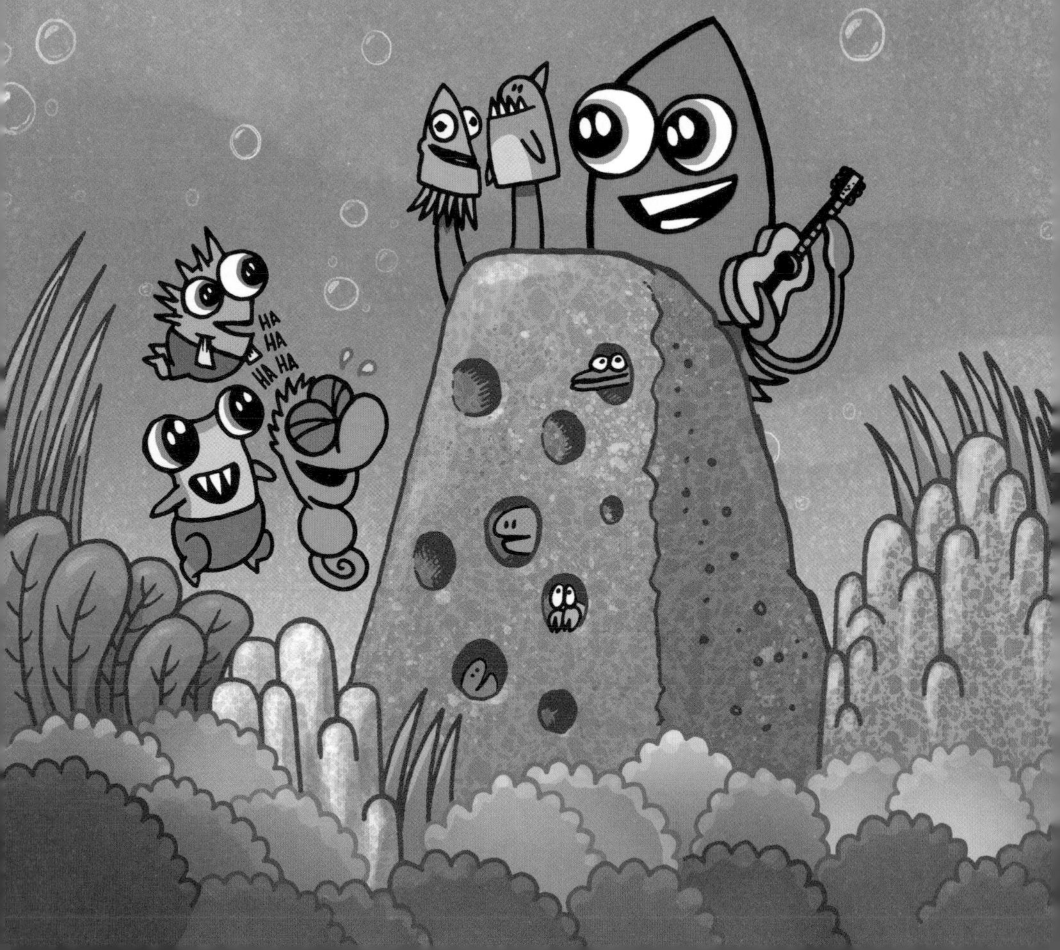
HA
HA
HA
HA